BRIDGEND LIBRARY

3 8030

CW00798026

The Hidden Apaches

Phil Roche, the foremost gambler on the Mississippi river-boats, was an exacting man. To cheat him and live, you had to be quicker on the draw. So far, nobody had been. But all that changed when he heard that Susan had been murdered and her child, Lucie, kidnapped. The Apaches seemed to be the prime suspects.

Now the people of Lanchester County would discover that Roche could be just as tough outside the casino. He would find Lucie despite the sheriff, the Bar Q ranch, the Army, and even Carlito's renegade Apaches. If he had killed over the turn of a card, what wouldn't he do for a missing child?

But Roche's search uncovers more than he had bargained for – about Lucie, about himself, and the secret of the Hidden Apaches. . . .

The Hidden Apaches

MIKE STALL

BRIDGEND LIBRARY AND INFORMATION SERVICE
GWASANAETH LLYFRGELL A GWYBODAETH PEN-Y-BONT AR OGWR

WITHDRAWN FROM STOCK
WEDI DILEU O STOC

PRICE
PRIS 20p

A Black Horse Western

ROBERT HALE · LONDON

© Mike Stall 2004
First published in Great Britain 2004

ISBN 0 7090 7495 6

Robert Hale Limited
Clerkenwell House
Clerkenwell Green
London EC1R 0HT

The right of Mike Stall to be identified as
author of this work has been asserted by him
in accordance with the Copyright, Designs and
Patents Act 1988.

BRIDGEND LIBRARY & INFORMATION SERVICE	
Cypher	31.07.04
	£10.75
0892/04	

Typeset by
Derek Doyle & Associates, Liverpool.
Printed and bound in Great Britain by
Antony Rowe Limited, Wiltshire

PROLOGUE

Roche was sure. The man was dealing from the bottom and quite skilfully. He glanced again at his own hand – two pair, good enough to bet on, obviously not good enough to win. He had thirty dollars in the pot but that hardly counted. He was being cheated. The rules were being broken. You didn't break the rules. They were gamblers and that was all that was left to them – the rules.

Roche glanced at the man, fat-faced with that porcine sort of arrogance that made his hackles rise, and prepared to call him out.

He'd called out men before. Sometimes

they went up on to the deck of the Mississippi steamboat to settle the matter; once they'd fought it out on a sandbar; but mostly it was done here in the gambling-rooms, quick and final, and the game continued with the smell of gunpowder in the air and a boy from the crew pouring wood-shavings over the blood.

It would be quick this time. The light in those piglike eyes would be out in less than a minute. Lucky man not to know that, he thought, and yet Roche felt a vast distaste for the act he was about to perform. That was because of the letter, the dry lawyer's letter in his jacket pocket telling him Susan was dead. Murdered at just twenty-seven, and his last words to her almost a curse.

'It's your call.'

Roche hesitated. Somehow he didn't want this man's life. And yet to let him go unchallenged was to break the rule he lived by. You gambled with more than money; your honour was at stake.

Except he knew now that it wasn't, that it never had been – that he had been playing a much bigger game than poker and that he would never play the lesser game again. It wasn't revenge that he wanted. She hadn't been his to avenge for many years now, but he had to know. He …

'It's your call, Roche.'

He looked up, saw the pig eyes break from his as if the man somehow knew just how close to death he had been. Roche smiled.

'I fold.'

1

The officer got on the stage at Mission Wells.

'In you go, Captain, I'll see to your luggage,' the driver said.

Roche, who had occupied the coach heretofore in solitary grandeur, looked over the newcomer. He was young, rather thin and very West Point. Roche's glance must have touched an instant too long on the single silver bar of his rank, for the newcomer said:

'I'm Lieutenant James, sir, not a captain at all.'

Roche smiled despite himself, recalling how irritating it was for a junior officer to be 'promoted' by a civilian, usually one trying to get a bigger tip. It never worked.

'Due and close attention to duty will no doubt amend that situation,' Roche said in the inimitable way of a senior officer joshing a junior. He regretted it instantly. Those days were well and truly gone. He offered his hand. 'I'm Phil Roche.'

'Alan James, sir,' the other said, taking it.

'For duty's sake, don't call me "sir". We've a fair journey ahead. I'll feel decrepit by the end of it if you do.' Even as he said it he knew he'd hit the same note again.

'You were in the army ... Phil?'

Roche nodded. 'All the same, I promise not to bore you with my tales of the war. Which, I believe, is an occupational hazard.'

James grinned. 'The uniform does sometimes bring back old memories.'

Suddenly the coach was in motion again. Roche extended a foot to the seat opposite to brace himself – they were running light in freight, too, and the coach was bouncy – and after a moment James, obviously wondering whether it was in the tradition of West Point and deciding it was, did likewise.

'Are you going to join your regiment?' Roche asked quickly, intent on moving away from the war and the past in general.

'In a way, sir... Phil.' James laughed, then: 'I'm taking up my first command.'

'Congratulations.'

'Oh, it's just a small fort with a reduced troop of horsed infantry – whatever that may turn out to mean – but...'

'It'll mean they can't ride and they're vastly understrength to boot,' Roche said; it was an easy prophecy.

'I reckon so...' James said, suddenly defensive.

'I'm not criticizing, Alan, just remembering.' He paused. 'I'll tell you this – you'll never have a command that you'll love better.'

James nodded, still too young to be easy about loving anything, even a reduced troop of horsed infantry.

'What's the fort's name?'

'Fort Bixbee.'

'After the general?' Roche asked,

suppressing a smile but not quite well enough. James noticed.

'He was no Napoleon but he won.'

That was at least half-right, Roche thought, and a small fort for horsed infantry seemed somehow appropriate and suitable for commemorating his achievements.

'Will we be neighbours, sir?'

Roche noticed the return of the honorific and the polite coolness that had suddenly descended on their forced acquaintance-ship.

'Just briefly. I've ... inherited some prop-erty thereabouts. I'm going there to settle matters.'

Roche turned slightly to glance out of the window on his side. The thin soil of the American South-west was mostly covered with a scant carpeting of grass that bore little relation to the lusher varieties back East. Cattle country at best but hardly the best cattle country either. He found himself thinking of Susan, that last brief meeting and the harsh words he'd spoken, the way he'd said he never wanted to see her again. Well, he hadn't, and their engagement broken, George Templeton had soon married her. Somehow it seemed they'd fetched up on a ranch of all places, and now he was dead and she'd been... murdered. Just a solitary word in the lawyer's letter and it had cut him like a knife. It paid to be very careful when you wished for something ... sometimes wishes really were granted.

'I'm sorry, sir,' James said suddenly, 'I shouldn't be so touchy.'

'Lieutenants are naturally touchy, captains skittish and only field officers have gravitas. Generals have gravitas and dignity both, though not much good does it do them.' He turned to look at the young officer. 'The fort's yours to make of it what you will. You'll do a good job, Alan, I'm sure of it.'

James suddenly slapped his thigh.

'You're that Roche – Colonel Philip Roche!'

Roche sighed. He hadn't intended to give himself away.

'Just Phil Roche now, if you please. You outrank me, Alan, and so do your corporals. I'd like to keep it that way.'

James looked disappointed but he

stopped pressing. He'd obviously looked Bixbee up on getting the command of 'his' fort and found Roche there too. The good bits. The bad bits, the career wrecking bits, hadn't gotten themselves in the record. Bixbee had been clever. If they had, they could have been questioned....

At Indio Stopover a Castilian-Mexican girl with her duenna joined the party. Their weight and more especially the weight of their luggage did much for the stability of the coach. Señorita de las Casas was a remarkable pretty young woman and Lieutenant James's attention was suitably diverted. She had no English but somehow James discovered that they had a common language in French which, remarkably, James spoke with some fluency and without the usual West Point nasality, which very obviously impressed both the duenna and her charge.

Roche was content to listen. It was a seduction scene where no one was in danger of being seduced, and it achieved its own somewhat stilted charm because of it. He was sorry when they arrived at

Hacienda del Sol and the pair descended to be replaced by a drummer, a woman with two fretful children and a silent man in black who was either a faro dealer or an itinerant preacher. But at least they kept the conversation away from military matters.

At last they arrived in Lanchester, the county seat, and the coach pulled up outside a clapboard 'Grand Hotel' which was probably the best in town, for the saloon bar was in the back, not in the front.

'You'll not forget your promise to visit?' James said.

'No,' Roche replied, having forgotten already that he'd promised anything. Had he? It hardly mattered. A waiting corporal was now in attendance and, handshakes over, both military men disappeared into the saloon.

Roche considered the delights of whiskey and conversation but rejected them. A soft bed was far more enticing. The stagecoach bench had been disturbingly hard and the rolling motion oddly like the sea. Maybe I'm getting old, he thought, but then that was probably just the contrast between Lieutenant James and himself. Envious? He considered the matter and decided not. He would not now like to be a soldier again, not a soldier without a war, for all its horrors.

'Can I get you anything, sir?' asked the bellboy who conducted him to his room. Despite his title he was an old, rather wizened little man with a leering look to him, but a bellboy of any description showed at least that the hotel had some pretensions to its proclaimed grandeur; Roche guessed that whores were admitted only via the back stairs.

'Yes,' he said, 'you can bring me a pint of whiskey. Just that.'

The ugly little creature set off on his errand, smiling slightly as if pleased that he had so easily winkled out Roche's vices. Wrongly. Roche drank little – gamblers who did drink rapidly became plain bums – but for once he fancied he needed alcohol's soporific effects to get any sleep. The motion of the coach had got into his bones.

Roche shaved himself in the soft morning

light. He hadn't bothered to call for hot water. He'd got used to cold water in the army. Oddly, the face in the mirror didn't look as old as he felt. He could hardly complain about that.

He glanced at the bottle of whiskey on the bedside table. It was hardly touched. He'd been more tired even than he'd thought. It was a long, long way here from St Louis.

He needed a bath too, but he wanted to get his business over and done with quickly, so he sponged himself down with a wet towel, getting the dust of travel off him. A meal would complete the job but he didn't feel hungry. He dressed in fresh clothes, leaving the others on the bed. He'd get the bellboy to arrange to have them washed. He hesitated a moment over the .32 he normally carried in a shoulder holster and decided against. It didn't seem necessary for a visit to a lawyer's office though he did keep his usual derringer. Discretion was one thing, nakedness another.

Lanchester wasn't much. There'd been nothing here before the Mexican war a generation back, not even a mission, and

17

all the buildings were of clapboard construction, which was a polite way of saying they were built like huts. But it was a county seat and had its city hall and two jails – the sheriff's and the marshal's. That seemed like too much law altogether but it didn't concern him. The lawyers' offices did. There were three of them all together by the city hall and Josiah Andrews' was the one in the centre.

Andrews was alone in the office, seated at a huge wooden desk flanked by wooden file cabinets. He looked up briefly.

'Yes?'

Roche looked him over carefully. He was oldish, a beefy-looking man going to seed but still not quite gone. There was nothing about him that said 'dishonest' and Roche, as a gambler, had got to be an excellent judge.

'You wrote to me concerning Mrs Templeton. I'm Philip Roche.'

Andrews half-rose from his seat, indicated a chair.

'I'd been awaiting your letter, sir. I did not expect to see you in person.'

Roche sat down. 'I want to know what happened.'

'Exactly as I put it in the letter. The property goes to you as set down in her will. The only other possible claimant was her daughter but alas—'

'There was a child?'

'Lucia. She was five years old.'

Roche went very cold. 'She was murdered too?'

'She's ... probably dead. No body was found but in the circumstances any coroner would certify her death.'

'What circumstances?'

'Mrs Templeton was killed by Apaches, sir – renegades under that devil Carlito.' He paused. 'Originally the ranch was the sole property of Mr Templeton but went to his wife on his death. Mrs Templeton left everything to you, not her daughter, with the hope, though not the proviso, that you would assume responsibility for her as her guardian. A little unusual but quite legal. As for the ranch—'

'Tell me about the child,' Roche said.

'There's little enough to tell. She's missing. The killing was done outdoors. It's more than likely both were killed at the same time and the child's body carried off by coyotes.'

'Don't Apaches ever steal children?'

'Yes, they do … but only boy children, to raise as their own.'

Roche was silent a moment, then: 'What happened to Templeton?' He hadn't fully accepted the death of the child, likely as it was, but he knew it was pointless to argue.

'He was dragged by his horse and killed,' Andrews said. 'That was six months back.'

'No Apaches involved?'

'They only started raiding six weeks ago. And they'll be in Mexico now in all probability.'

'So the three deaths together are pure coincidence?' Roche knew he was reaching but noticed that Andrews didn't hasten to pooh-pooh the implication. Eventually he said:

'It's unusual but such things happen.'

They did, Roche knew, more often even than Andrews guessed. There was just one more thing to ask.

'Are there any takers for the ranch?'

'The Bar Q has made a provisional offer.'

'How much?'

'Three thousand dollars.'

'Is that fair?'

'I might get them up a few hundred. Do you want me to try?'

'Not for the moment.' He made to get up. 'I'll be back.'

Andrews stayed him with a gesture. 'There's one more thing, sir. I said I hadn't expected you here but Mrs Templeton did. She left a letter to be given to you if the will were ever to be ... needed. Nor were you to be advised of its existence should you not come personally.' He reached into a drawer and produced a wax sealed envelope. 'She assured me it wasn't a legal document but if you wish me to see it—'

'I doubt there'll be need,' Roche said. He reached across, took it and slipped it into his pocket. A personal letter out of the past was something he would have done without. He'd read it later.

Out on the sidewalk he stopped and caught his breath. There had been almost too much to take in – so Susan and Templeton had had a child! He'd never even thought of her being a mother and yet what was more natural? And then to find that the child was very probably dead....

He needed a drink but not alone in his room. He glanced across the street and saw a sign that read: O'GRADY'S TAVERN. He started across.

Roche stared at his barely touched whiskey, remembering. Those had been bad days for him: his army career had been almost on the rocks but he might still have fought back, maybe even retrieved it. Being in the right didn't harm at all, though it was no guarantee of success either. But it was Susan's reaction that had really hurt. Almost inconceivably, his fianceé had cast him off. Perhaps under family pressure but...?

What did it matter? Why was he here at all? And how had she known he'd come? Maybe there would be answers in the letter but he wasn't sure he wanted to know them. He certainly didn't want the ranch. And why leave it to him and not her own daughter? Had she expected something else would happen?

Someone jostled his arm. He looked to his left and saw the cowboy leaning on the bar, gesturing to the barman.

'Another bottle.'

'Sure thing, Mr Morton,' the barman said.

Roche looked away but Morton had noticed his glance.

'Who the hell are you?'

'Just a fellow drinker.'

'Hell, I don't like your face, fellow drinker,' Morton said.

For a moment Roche had thought he was drunk but then realized he wasn't – not quite. Morton was in the mood to show off. To whom was also obvious. They were a couple of cowboys at a nearby table looking on, both hardly more than boys. Neither was armed but Morton was, with a fancy two-gun rig.

Roche knew the scenario well. He was meant to grovel, then retreat. Morton had no intention of shooting him. He'd been picked because he wasn't wearing an obvious gun. Morton thought him unarmed. You got hanged for shooting unarmed men but not for overawing them.

Walk away? Why not, he'd almost finished his drink? But he wasn't exactly in the mood to walk away. He found himself regretting not wearing the .32. It was mistake he'd not make again, either way.

'Take your bottle and stop bothering me,' he said mildly. The barman had arrived and was proffering the bottle. Morton ignore him.

'Just because you haven't got the guts to wear a gun, don't think—'

Roche cut him short. 'If you want a fight, let's step out into the street and I'll kill you there.' He'd spoken softly but it wasn't meant for the soft answer that turned away wrath. Only a fool would doubt that he meant every word.

Morton wasn't quite that.

'Heck, mister, just joshing,' he said quickly, all thought of boasting forgotten. It was the way Roche had talked about killing that got to him. Not a threat but a cold statement. The fact that he carried no visible gun hardly mattered. Morton somehow knew the stranger would kill him and think no more of it than *he* did of shooting a prairie dog. Less. He did that for fun. The stranger didn't look like he'd get any fun out of it at all.

'Your bottle,' Roche said, gesturing slightly.

Morton took the bottle and retreated to the table. The bar had suddenly gone quiet, not out of anticipation for no one expected violence now, but death had been very close and everyone knew it, Morton most of all.

Roche finished his drink and left.

Roche put off reading the letter as long as he could, wandering about town, taking his meal in the small Mexican quarter, of *burritos* that might have had some connection with *burros*, even taking a siesta in the afternoon heat. But at last, as the lamps were flaring in the street outside, he could put it off no long. He sat on his bed, tore open the letter and read:

My Dearest Philip,
If you are reading this it is because I am dead and for all you have every right not to care – I treated you abominably – you care still. When your army career ran into trouble my parents made me break our engagement. I should never have let

them, not only because it was wrong but because I loved you. Yet I was weak. And then I found out something that terrified me and I was weak again: I married George Templeton apparently 'on the rebound' ... which was horribly unfair to him too. And as if in judgement he and his family lost their fortune in a stock swindle only a year later, so we came out here to the only property remaining to him – but it was a judgement on me, not him.

I write this after his death which has been called an accident. I do not believe that, though in this I can hardly expect you to care. But if I go down that same road, as I fear I may, my daughter Lucie will be left unprotected and this you will care about when I tell you that – but you have guessed already. And perhaps suspect that I was lying. Why not? I betrayed you, I betrayed George, who knew in his heart that Lucie was not his but yours. God help me, he loved me despite my faults!

I'm sorry, Philip, so sorry for everything and for laying a further burden upon you. You have every right not to accept it but knowing you I can rest a

little easier for having penned these words which I truly hope you will never read. But if you are reading them now, forgive me if you can. I've found it hard to forgive myself if only because I have always remained
  Your loving
  Susan.

Roche's first inclination was to disbelieve, but it could all be true. They had made love and used the fact of war to justify themselves, and that had made him all the more bitter against her later. He could check the dates...

But there was no need. It wasn't a lie and he knew it. It positively rang with bitter truth. God help him, she'd still loved him despite herself, nursed his child while married to a man she hadn't loved, but who loved her. She asked forgiveness and that was easy to grant, empty as it was, and yet it was a burden lifted – the bitterness that had soured him all these years was gone. He pitied her now. Her worst betrayal had been of herself. As for the child...

His child! The letter was a revenant

27

from the past but Lucie was here and now and was his.

And missing!

How casually Andrews had said that word, and how casually he'd taken it! But if she were alive then the whole damned mess made some kind of sense, his life made some kind of sense ... but to find out he had a daughter and then discover that she was probably dead...

No. That was a foolish phrase. You were either alive or you were dead. Susan had given Lucie into his care and he could not write her off for a lawyer's casual phrasing.

He felt emotion the like of which he'd never known and it almost overwhelmed him. His child!

His living child. She was that and he'd find her, find her alive and not only for Susan but for himself.

The emotion surged over him and at the same time he felt a terrible purpose growing within him, a purpose the like of which he had not felt since the war. And this was stronger by far. He'd find Lucie, God help him, and he'd find her alive. Time enough later to think of what would happen should he find her dead. That would be the time for tears and they surely would not be his alone.

2

Dasinger pointed to the rise that he'd previously dignified with the name of hill. The Templeton ranch ran from there to the stand of trees yonder. His arm moved in an almost grandiloquent gesture. Roche had consulted the land office map Andrews had sent over to his room along with a copy of the will and knew the whole amounted to 2,000 acres, which sounded a very great deal, but not when the grass was as sparse as this and saguaro cacti were more in evidence than cattle.

'It's not bad land for cattle,' Dasinger went on, 'if you work at it. I used to be a top hand on the old Zeeboom spread and

31

we raised a thousand head on not much more.'

'What happened to that?'

'The Bar Q bought it up, after...' He broke off.

'After what?'

'Zeeboom got bit by a rattler.'

'And died?'

'He got bit in the neck.'

'The Bar Q wants to buy this spread,' Roche said neutrally.

'Yeah, they'll end up owning the whole valley.'

'And people keep dying around them.'

Dasinger didn't reply or meet his eyes. 'The ranch house is—'

'Just past the draw, over there on your left.'

'I thought you'd never been here before,' Dasinger said.

'I saw the map.'

'Yeah, I heard talk in town you were ex-army. Looked more like a gambler to me but I reckon I guessed wrong. Officer?'

Roche nodded. 'I have played the odd hand of poker too.'

'Do you want me to go back?'

'I paid you to take me to the ranch

house, didn't I?'

'Surely.' Dasinger started down the draw. He was an old man on an old horse, and even that was not his own. The owner of the livery stable had recommended him as a guide. Roche had guessed that he was, if not exactly the town drunk, not one of its soberest citizens either. Roche urged his own horse, itself no Arabian, to catch up, so they rode spur to spur.

'You know why I'm here?'

'Mrs Templeton left you the ranch.'

'That's not what I care about. If Carlito's Apaches killed her, I'll see them hang. If anyone else...' He paused, then: 'I'll pay well for information.'

Dasinger shook his head, then: 'At least, you haven't threatened me.'

'I don't know enough yet to threaten anyone. If I did, I might.'

Dasinger smiled, an old man's smile. Roche didn't press him further. Dasinger hadn't refused to help exactly. It was best to leave it at that for now.

The ranch house was a shock, a big adobe structure that had once been lime-washed but was now reverting to the colour of mud. It looked almost as if the rain would wash it away, if it ever rained in these parts. The barn was of like construction; the corral was of wood but ancient, dried-out wood, 'patched' here and there with rope. Both barn and corral were empty. Roche glanced at Dasinger.

'The horses are at the Bar Q – it ain't unusual. There was nobody here to feed 'em so the neighbours took 'em in. They'll give 'em back for the asking.'

'And the stock?'

'Out on the range, grubbing grass with the rest. They'll be sorted out at round up. Nobody cheats.'

Roche nodded, then: 'Wait here. I'll look inside.'

The interior was cool and dank and dusty. Roche guessed that nothing had been stolen for there was nothing to steal – a single crude wardrobe holding a man's suit, three full-sized dresses and four that would fit a child. There was one bonnet. In the kitchen, which had no pump, there was an empty stone sink, a rusty stove and a shelf holding a single set of cracked pottery. In the main room a travelling-clock was silent, gathering dust. The furniture was all local and crude, including the redwood table which even now had a hint of beeswax polish smell to it.

Had Susan lived here all these years, getting poorer and poorer as outside the cattle starved for want of rain and grass, all the while toiling with her own hands to raise a child and feed a family? It was scarcely believable. Back East she'd been all flounces and bonnets and as flighty as propriety allowed.

Roche stood by the fireplace, its grate now a dried-orange colour from disuse, and glanced at the pictures on the mantelpiece; a studio photograph of Templeton and Susan, she with a baby in her arms, and a portrait of a small girl in a cheap dress looking shyly at the camera. He stared at the features but saw nothing of himself, just another child. He reached out, took the photograph from its cheap frame and put it in his pocket. He took a deep breath then walked quickly out into the daylight.

He found Dasinger at the back of the house by the well, pouring a bucket of water into the horse trough. He let the bucket down again – by hand, for there was no windlass. It took a long time before it hit water.

'How do you live in this land?'

'With difficulty,' Dasinger said. 'We're having a dry spell now but when the rains come, the land's as green as Vermont. In a bad time, you just stick it out.'

He'd misjudged Dasinger, he realized. He might be down on his luck but that was all. He said:

'Where was she found?'

'Here, by the well.'

There was nothing to see, no bloodstains left. It was too dry and dusty for that.

'You saw her?'

Dasinger nodded. 'It's a small town. Most of us came out.' He paused. 'She'd been shot, nothing else. There was no sign at all of that kind.'

Roche was silent for a moment, then: 'Would the Apaches have guns?'

Dasinger looked at him patiently. 'It's the first thing they buy, borrow or steal. Hell, if they still used bows and arrows would we need a fort?' He turned his attention back to the well, drawing up another half-full bucket. The heat and the horses had reduced the contents of the first to a damp stain on the parched wood of the shallow trough.

'So you reckon it was Apaches?'

Dasinger poured out the water. 'I wasn't here.'

Roche didn't press him. He looked back at the house, noticed a small lean-to against the back wall. He gestured at it questioningly.

'You could say that's the bunkhouse.'

Roche walked over and put his head inside. It was quite empty – not even a rag. It would have housed one, two at most.

'Who stayed here?' he asked Dasinger who was leading up the horses.

'They sometimes had a Mexican to help out with the herd. Domingo. An old man.'

'Was he here that day?'

'His body wasn't found,' Dasinger said, 'so I reckon not.'

' "Mexican" can mean a lot of things.'

'Surely, but he was no Apache if that's what you're thinking. And if you want to know how I know, it's easy. Your scalp itches when there are Apaches around, believe me.' He paused, then: 'Do you want to go on to the Bar Q and see about your remuda?

Roche shook his head. 'Not today. Besides, I reckon they'll be coming to see me.'

'You could very well be right,' Dasinger said, mounting up.

The hotel room had become oppressively small. The moonlight seeped coldly in through the poorly curtained windows and the thin walls had proved to be no better at keeping out the bitter cold of the night than they were with the oppressive heat of the day.

He'd slept briefly and dreamed alarmingly. The only image he retained was of a bundle of bloody rags by a well....

He got up and pulled off the useless curtains. Moonlight flooded into the room, almost bright enough to read by. He got back into bed and pulled up the blankets.

It had seemed so much easier back on the Mississippi. He'd imagined that the cloud of unknowing would have dispersed long before this point. But it hadn't. It was hard to believe that anyone would kill for that achingly dry ranch house and range, yet murder had been done. He tried to establish a list of possibles in his mind in order of probability but it was impossible to choose between them. Apaches? Maybe, but no one had seen them. The Bar Q? But a woman on her own out there was going to fail anyway so why anticipate? A passing drifter? As faceless as the Apaches.

He reached for the bottle of whiskey, thought better of it. Instead he picked up the photograph of the child which lay beside it.

She didn't look particularly like Susan either. She just looked like any common or garden five-year-old, a babyish pudginess still hiding the family face.

Alive or dead? The odds were long against the former but he somehow didn't believe in them. Why carry off a child you intended to kill? As for the coyote theory, he'd questioned Dasinger and no tracks had been seen. He would have liked to push the matter further but hadn't because the old man had been so obviously reluctant to talk against the Bar Q. Roche had hoped it was them. Apaches were ghosts but the Bar Q was real and if it was their work there was a chance Lucie was alive somewhere. Surely it took more than land greed to kill a five year old child?

But he needed to go carefully, legally if he could. Back in the saloon with the bullying cowboy he'd been brave enough because he really hadn't given a damn either way. Now he did. He had a daughter and nothing in the world was going to stop him finding her.

He set the photograph down and lay back. He'd sleep now, and somehow he knew he would have no more bad dreams.

When in doubt, try city hall. But it wasn't advice that was likely to catch on, Roche thought, as he waited in the small outer office under the stare of a deputy whose duties seemed to consist solely in sitting with his feet on the desk smoking hand-rolled cigarettes.

It was probably as well no more was asked of him as the man was extraordinarily fat. He wore no gunbelt though a Navy Colt lay on the desk within easy reach. Roche didn't underestimate him – he'd be a dangerous man, at night, behind you.

'We were all sorry about Mrs Templeton,' he said, flicking his ash on the floor. 'If'n I had my way, we'd settle them red devils once for all.'

Roche said nothing. He doubted any Indian with two good feet, let alone a horse, had anything to fear from Deputy Horace Cable.

Eventually there was a tapping on the ceiling.

'He'll see you now,' Cable said. 'Up the stairs, first on your right.'

Roche went up the stairs, catching a sight of the cells in the back through a peephole cut in the wall. There were just two of them, both small and empty. He came to the door and rapped on it.

'Come on in.'

Sheriff Crown was very different from his deputy; he looked like a snake-oil salesman made good, all oily political charm and glad-handing.

'Sorry to keep you waiting, sir. Terrible business about Mrs Templeton and her kid.'

'And her husband.'

'That was an accident.'

'A coincidence all the same.'

Crown shrugged. 'This is a hard land. Hell, you've seen it for yourself.'

'How are your investigations proceeding?' Roche asked softly.

'Investigations? As for Templeton, accidents happen, as I just said. And as for Susan Templeton and the kid, Apaches are the army's business.' Again the politician's smile but dismissive this time.

There would be no help from Sheriff Crown, Roche decided as he walked back to his hotel. Crown hadn't exactly warned him off but he'd put up the shutters all the same. Had someone told him to? Just who had put Crown into office? He could hazard a guess easily enough but it didn't prove anything. Nobody liked people nosing about their business and anyway there was a good chance no orders had actually been given. The likes of Crown greased their way up by anticipating requests, and sometimes they got it wrong too. He'd seen that in other small towns. Once you'd bought the law you ended up with idiots with badges.

Maybe he'd do better with the local newspaper office and he was turning in that direction when he almost walked into the girl.

She was coming out of the general store laden with boxes, a hatbox on top, and as she stopped abruptly it fell and bounced across the sidewalk, only to be eventually halted by the wheel of the rig parked right by. Roche bent to retrieve it.

'Thanks,' she said, her face now revealed by the box's absence. It was a remarkably pretty face surmounted by dark lustrous hair and inset with lively dark-blue eyes.

'My pleasure, ma'am. Can I help you with those?'

'If you could put the top two on the rig ...'

Roche obliged and when she had deposited the rest with them she smiled at him.

'Thank you again.'

'Light work, ma'am.'

'Please call me Helen. The "ma'am" makes me feel old.'

'You've no occasion to worry ... Helen.' He paused, then: 'I'm Phil Roche.'

'Ah, the mysterious stranger!' She laughed. 'I'm sorry but this is a small town.'

'I like small towns,' Roche said gallantly.

They were interrupted by the arrival of a middle-aged man in a well-cut dark suit and a rather Eastern looking hat.

'I'm sorry, my dear, but Mr Johnson delayed me in the shop. Did you manage?'

'With Mr Roche's aid, Father.' She turned to Roche, smiling again. 'Mr Roche, this is my father, William Quinn.'

'The new owner of the Templeton place?' Quinn asked, extending his hand. 'I'm pleased to meet you, sir. Terrible business, terrible.'

Roche took it, a little amazed. This was the leader of the Bar Q brand, this gunless milquetoast of a man?

'Indeed,' he said.

'As we're neighbours now, or will be when you move in, you must come to visit us at the Bar Q. Come to dinner. No need to drive back in the dark, either. We've plenty of rooms. Tomorrow, say?'

'You're rushing the poor man!' Helen said, laughing.

Roche smiled at her. 'Not at all. It's always good to get to know your neighbours. I'll be happy to accept.'

'Then it's decided,' William Quinn said. 'It'll be a pleasure for me and give my daughter the chance to wear some of these fancy clothes she's bought.'

'Father!'

'You look lovely to me in dungarees, my dear,' Quinn said equably. 'This young man might think differently, of course, which will put you on your mettle.'

'Your daughter would grace anything,' Roche said, a little bemused. The conspiracy he'd half-imagined had collapsed utterly. The Bar Q as represented by William Quinn could hardly be an actor in the scenario he'd devised.

'Six, then. We dine early. I'll look forward to it. Now sir, we'd better be getting back. I've tally sheets to go over and Helen here will have feminine things to do, I'm sure.'

Roche watched them drive off sedately looking every bit like an Episcopalian minister and his daughter in a New English town. His previous intention of visiting the local press baron hardly seemed important now but he had a job to do and, despite the bizarre encounter, it was no less urgent than before.

The *Lanchester City & County News* occupied a tiny building just off Main Street. It was dominated by a small, ancient press and presided over by an editor, printer and distributor all rolled into one – Red Walters, whose once distinguishing hair had long since faded from fire to ice.

'Heard about the way you faced down young Morton, sent him scuttling back to the Bar Q with his tail between his legs. Good work. Do him good too. One of these days he'd've met up with someone less merciful than you.'

Merciful! It had been precisely the lack of it that Morton had recognized and which had sent him crawling back to his buddies. Roche had been ready to kill and Morton had known it. But there was no reason to tell Walters that. Instead he asked about Lucie and Susan.

'Odd business,' Walters said. 'Apaches don't steal girl children and neither do they carry off their bodies.'

'Coyotes?' Roche asked, almost choking on the word.

'Ditto. And carry off to where? No, it wasn't coyotes. She just disappeared. A plain dang mystery.'

'Then you think she's dead?'

Walters considered the matter, then:

'It's probable but who can say for sure? Not knowing's not knowing, and there's a fact!'

'I want to know.'

He must have said that with more force than he intended because he noticed Walters looking at him carefully. If it would have helped Lucie, Roche would have told the whole county whose daughter she really was, but it wouldn't so he just said:

'Susan Templeton was a dear friend of my family.'

'Reckon so, making you her heir.' He thought the matter over. 'The best I can offer is to put a notice in the paper.'

'Would a reward help?'

'It usually does. How much?'

Roche considered. His bank account was substantial. Not having cared too much about money, it had come to him easily. And nobody had ever cheated him.

'A thousand dollars?'

'Phew, that's big money. It might do no good but it'd set ears pricking, no doubt about that.'

'Then set it up. How much do I owe you?'

'I'll send a bill.' Walters looked at him. 'You're more interested in the girl than the ranch, aren't you?"

'A matter of honour,' Roche said. 'The will laid me under an obligation.'

'Sure.' Walters paused. 'I hear you tried your luck with our esteemed county sheriff.'

Roche nodded.

'An ineffectual man, our sheriff,' Walters said. 'But he's not the law officer for the city. We have a marshal for that.'

'Not, I heard, at the moment.'

'That's true, and I especially regret the fact in my other capacity, of which you seem to be unaware.'

Roche looked a question.

'Mayor. Any man who owns a newspaper and can't get himself elected to something is a damned fool.' He paused. 'A man asking questions gets better answers when he has some reason for doing so, some status. How about it?'

No. The word formed on Roche's lips but he didn't utter it. A city marshal's authority was severely limited but for most people a badge was a badge. And the duties wouldn't be very onerous. It might just give him an edge. He seemed to be getting nowhere fast as it was. He said:

'I might help out for a while, until you can get someone permanent.'

Walters delved into his pocket, produced a key which he tossed to Roche. 'Now, raise your right hand.'

Roche did so.

'Do you swear to uphold the laws of this city and the Constitution of the United States, so help you God?'

'I do.'

'Then you're now marshal. There's a badge and six-gun in the office. The salary—'

'Won't be required. Let's just say it's mutually convenient.'

'I won't argue with that, and neither will the city council.'

'I'll be out of town tomorrow night,' Roche said. 'I'm visiting the Bar Q.' He paused. 'I'd wondered about the Bar Q, then I met William Quinn ...'

Walters laughed. 'And you thought he ran the Bar Q?'

'He doesn't?' Roche asked sharply.

'He's half-owner. The other half's owned by his brother Harry, a very different kind of man, believe me.'

'What kind of man is that?'

Walters smiled. 'I'll leave you to find that out for yourself.'

3

Roche looked at the heavy Colt six-gun
and decided against. He'd carried and
used the like in the war but there had
never been any occasion when a quick
draw was required and he'd be slower
with it than a tiro. Better stick to what he
had. There was also a Greener shotgun
which had been cut down to half-length to
make a very useful riot gun. There were
cartridges too and a holster. He decided
against the holster: if he ever needed it,
the best place to carry it was in the hand.
It would cut down arguments no end.

The marshal's office was small, the size
of a regular store and that cut in half to

make room for the single, empty cell. Nobody had reinforced the cell's walls, so you could cut your way out with a penknife, but it would suffice as a drunk tank. There was a desk and a chair too, a few ancient 'dodgers' – wanted posters – in the drawers along with a pint bottle of whiskey, empty. Nothing else. Not even a law book but the technicalities of the law weren't too worrisome west of the Pecos, he knew. You just kept the peace as best you could.

Not that he cared too much about that. He would do it because he'd taken the oath but his real business was Lucie. And he was no nearer to finding her than he'd been the day he'd stepped off the stage, not even knowing he had a daughter. It was a sobering thought that if he hadn't come here, he'd never even have known.

Did he wish that? He sat by the desk and took out the photograph. She looked no different, still a little camera-shy in her best dress, one he couldn't even guess the colour of. Yet somehow she didn't 'feel' dead to him. He knew it was irrational but he felt that if she were dead, he'd know it. She was alive and waiting for him without knowing she was waiting.

'I'll find you,' he said softly, and knew he would. Whatever the cost, whatever it took. It wasn't a promise, it was more than that. It was now his credo.

'Look where you're going, girl,' William Quinn said sharply, a rarity for him. 'And slow down.'

Helen eased back on the reins and twitched the horses into the centre of the trail. She hadn't been thinking of her driving at all.

'Sorry, Daddy.'

William Quinn smiled. 'You're in dream, girl, have been since you met that handsome stranger.'

'You thought he was handsome?'

'Enough! See to your horses.' But he soon relented. 'I'd say so. A gentleman too, at least by—'

'Lanchester standards!' Helen laughed. After a moment: 'You seemed to know him.'

'Of him, rather. He's the new owner of the Templeton ranch. Poor Susan left it to him. Family friend, they say.'

Trust Father to know the town gossip.

Even on a short trip he managed to visit every bar in town.

And as co-owner of the Bar Q, people were only too anxious to get on his good side, even though most knew it was Harry Quinn who made the real decisions. Helen didn't particularly like this state of affairs but she'd grown up with it, seen her father a little more rum-soaked year on year and Harry that much stronger and more dominant.

But he'd never tried to dominate her. It was almost as if she had two fathers. Harry, unmarried, thought of her as his heiress, she knew. William Quinn had once said that his brother hadn't married because it would have been bigamy – his true wife was the Bar Q. And there was truth in that. It had more than tripled in size under Uncle Harry and was the biggest spread in the county. All the same it would have been better if father had some part in it. Not that he seemed to care.

She thought again about Roche. It had been just a casual meeting in the street, a minor act of courtesy, and yet there was something about him that intrigued her.

She was glad her father had invited him to the ranch and gladder that he'd accepted. Most people kept away because they knew Harry didn't really like visitors. But Roche either didn't know or didn't care. Both perhaps: he didn't know and wouldn't care if he did.

'He didn't have the look of a rancher,' she said.

'Oh, it's Roche again,' her father said tolerantly. 'No, I reckon not. Andrews could tell you, no doubt, but he's a close-mouthed old rascal, and the town gossips haven't had time to get to work on him yet. But I'd say Roche's a soldier.'

'Oh, so was everybody.'

'A lot of people have worn a uniform,' William Quinn conceded, 'but that young fellow was a soldier, and a good one.' He paused. 'Have a care before you set your cap at him, young lady. He's not like the young beaux you have around here, all ready to dance to your tune.'

'I don't have a single beau and you know it,' Helen said.

William Quinn laughed. 'As you will, my dear, as you will. But you do have admirers. And even if you weren't pretty you would still have them. Rather, the Bar Q would.'

'You think he admires the Bar Q?'

Her father was silent for a moment. 'I don't think he'd give a second's thought to it. If he likes you, it's you he likes.'

Helen found herself immensely pleased by that. Her father might hit the bottle too often but he was an excellent judge of character. Even Uncle Harry agreed to that.

But did Philip Roche like her? she asked herself. They'd exchanged hardly more than a glance. And yet somehow she felt he did. He'd agreed to visit them without hesitation. But he was from back East and invitations meant less there.

Suddenly they were over the last rise and the buildings of the Bar Q were blazing white before them in the afternoon sun.

The lights were beginning to flare in the street as the saloonkeepers lit their exterior lanterns, effectively lighting the whole street. Lanchester didn't have the newfangled gas lighting yet but Roche had no doubt it would arrive in due course, along with finger bowls and china crockery.

Law it already had, in the person of himself, and while he didn't know much about marshalling, he did know it was usual for the marshal to inspect his city in the morning and late evening. Which was to say, now. He had to show his face and thus the face of the law.

Why did I take the job? he asked himself. Was he so fond of authority that even the small amount provided by a marshal's badge was important to him? No. More likely, the mayor had seen him coming.

All the same, he had taken the job and it was his duty to carry it out. He considered what weapons to take. The six-gun would be useful, in his hand, but he was a legitimate law officer in a peaceful town, not a guard in some hellhole of a prison. That ruled out the sawn-off too. He was wearing his .32. That would suffice. Not that he expected to need it. He hadn't been long enough in Lanchester to make many enemies and the patrons of the various saloons hadn't had time enough to get fighting drunk yet. When a man was mad drunk and shooting up the town that was the time to sober him up quickly by showing him the muzzle of a sawn-off, not now.

He stood up, picked up his hat from the desk and started out on the first of his nightly rounds.

Main Street was wide and as the horsed traffic had seemingly ceased for the day the temptation was to walk down the very centre ... but it would make him too good a target. He kept to the right side of the street, which had the fewest saloons and oil-lamps, and opened his jacket to give him readier access to his .32.

Everything seemed quiet. The saloons, for all they blazed welcomingly with light, were relatively empty. Only on Saturday nights would they be packed, especially once a month after pay-day. That was when profits would really be made; now they were just going through the motions. Just like himself.

He heard the shuffling of boots on the wooden sidewalk across the street, not the sound of a man walking but of one changing position. As if to fire. He turned, saw something metal glint in the entrance of an alley and flung himself down just as he heard the crack! of the discharge. The bullet hit the wall of the building behind him – the land office, he noticed – just about at heart height. Roche kept low, unmoving. There had hardly been a fraction of a second between him falling and the shot. It was just possible that the assassin thought he'd already done his job. The mind played odd tricks in that kind of excitement. Besides, his only alternative was to charge across an open street into a dark alley. He eased the .32 into his hand and waited.

He was right. The would-be killer wasn't sure. He came out cautiously, the gun still in his hand, looking across the street. Roche didn't move. He didn't particularly want to kill him. He might know something, and anyway the .32 was more effective close up.

It was Morton, the gunhand who'd unsuccessfully braced him in the bar. The other six-gun of his extravagant rig was still housed on his hip, not unexpectedly. Two-handed draws were only for dime novels.

But Morton hadn't done all that badly.

Roche knew that if he hadn't reacted instantly, he would be dead. He'd come very close indeed. Morton truly was a gunhand of sorts. Most cowboys were terrible shots with handguns for all it was the fashion to wear them. Probably not very fast though, or he would have pushed harder that morning.

Roche was in no doubt that this was more than revenge for that. You didn't kill a man wearing a star without a very good reason, and Morton could hardly boast of the crime to revive his rep, not if he valued his neck. Roche didn't doubt that Morton wanted him dead, but somebody had paid him. And they might know something about Lucie.

Morton lowered his gun as he walked across the street, sure now that he'd already done the job. Yet he needed to make sure absolutely. But by the time he'd reached the edge of the sidewalk the gun was parallel with his leg. It was only then that Roche raised himself using his left arm and pointed the .32.

'Drop the gun,' he said.

Shocked, Morton did so. It fell on to the hard-packed dry earth of the street.

'Unbuckle your belt and drop it.' Then, still keeping his gun levelled, Roche slowly got to his feet.

It was a mistake. Seeing an opportunity Morton let his right hand snake across from the buckle to the butt of the second gun. He must have kept the holster well oiled for despite being the wrong way round for him he still managed to catch hold of it, flinging himself sideways as he tried to bring it to bear.

Roche took no chances and fired, but aiming for the right arm rather than a body shot. He wanted Morton alive.

There was nothing fake about the way Morton lay. He'd been hit. Roche stepped down from the sidewalk and bent over him. Morton's own movement had put his chest rather than his arm in the way of the .32 slug but at least it had missed his heart. He was alive.

Roche looked up. There were a dozen or so spectators gathered outside the saloon opposite.

'Come over and give me a hand to get him to the doctor's office.'

There was no shortage of volunteers.

Doc Huggett came out of the back of his office rattling something metallic in an iron kidney-dish.

'Yours, Marshal. Want it back?'

Roche ignored the old man's gallows humour.

'How is he?'

'Alive for the moment but not much longer. I couldn't stanch the wound.'

Maybe the old butcher had made matters worse but no good would come of saying so.

'Can he talk?'

Huggett shook his head. 'He's unconscious, for which he ought to be very grateful. His lungs are filling up with blood. Not a good way to go, believe me.'

'Are there any?' Mayor Walters asked. He was standing with three other spectators just inside the office, the rest having gone back to the saloons.

'I can think of one,' Huggett said, smiling unprofessionally.

'Leave it,' Walters said.

Huggett nodded. 'I'll go check on him.' He went again into the surgery and came out almost immediately. 'He's no longer my concern. It's the city coroner's. Isn't that one of your jobs, Mayor? Want to go see him?'

'I'll take your word,' Walters said.

'Earn your money, Mayor,' one of the spectators said.

'Later,' Walters replied with distaste.

'Let's clear the office,' Roche said, coming to his aid. No one was in the mood to defy him and they were turning to leave when Sheriff Crown arrived with his grossly fat deputy.

'This is city business!' Walters snapped at him by way of greeting.

'A killing is out of your purview, I believe,' Sheriff Crown replied. He looked at Roche. 'I heard you did it.'

Roche nodded. 'He took a shot at me from across the street as I was making my rounds, then came across to finish me off. He drew again but I was faster.'

The sheriff glanced at the badge on Roche's coat.

'Congratulations on your appointment, Marshal Roche, but killing's a county matter. I'll have your gun and you'll walk with me to my jail.'

That was totally unexpected. Roche had no idea of who was right in law but he knew it was unheard of to arrest a law officer in these circumstances. Walters thought so too.

'City business, I said. Besides, it was self-defence.'

'You got a witness, Mr Mayor?' Crown smiled.

Roche suddenly didn't care who was right in law. Of one thing he was certain, he wasn't going to any jail run by Crown.

'He has – the best.'

'Where is he?'

'You're listening to him. If you say otherwise I'll take it you're saying I'm a liar. I wouldn't care to have my honour impugned, Sheriff Crown. I'd demand satisfaction. Now, say, out in the street.'

Crown went white.

'I'm calling you out in front of witnesses,' Roche said, pressing him hard. 'It'll be a fair fight, just the two of—'

'Hey, wait a minute! Maybe I was too hasty.'

'You mean you're certain it was self-defence? You're saying that now in the presence of Mayor Walters and these witnesses?'

'Yeah, sure. Self-defence. I was just

being …' He broke off, then: 'I wasn't calling you a liar, no sir!'

'Then you've no further business here.'

'No sir,' the sheriff agreed and left abruptly; his deputy was already long gone.

Walters laughed. 'Hell, you sure put him to rights.'

'There'll be no comebacks?'

Walters shook his head decisively. 'He'll walk very softly around you from now on. He's a good man for collecting taxes is our sheriff, but that's about all. And you really had him believing you'd kill him.'

Because I would have, Roche thought. He had a job to do and nobody was about to get in his way. But there was no point telling Walters that.

'Let's go get ourselves a drink,' the mayor said after a moment.

'Why did he want to kill me?'

Walters already had two whiskeys under his belt and was about to down a third.

'You humiliated him. It was a back-shooter's revenge.'

'I don't buy that.'

'What does it matter? He's dead and Sheriff Crown has been well and truly put in his place. No sand. He ran like a little girl from a spider.'

Roche no longer gave a damn about the sheriff. At least in the short run there was no more to fear from him and that was all he cared about. The local rivalries between city and county could go hang.

'Who did you say Morton worked for?'

'You remember very well. He was a Bar Q man.'

'Interesting. I'm visiting the Bar Q tomorrow, staying overnight.'

'Hell no! You've killed one of theirs. They …' He broke off.

'I doubt it,' Roche said, anticipating his thought. 'Nobody mourns a dead gunhand. Even if I'm wrong, I've given my word.' He paused. 'I might be a few days. You'll be OK with the sheriff?'

Walters almost cackled. 'He'll keep his head well down for a long, long while.'

'Don't humiliate him in print,' Roche said suddenly.

'Why not?'

'The word will get around anyway, won't it?'

'Of course.'

'So he's hurt come the next election already. Save the other barrel, keep it in reserve, have something to hold over him.'

Walters clapped him on the back. 'You're right, young feller. You ought to be in politics. Hell, you will be!'

Roche didn't disabuse him of the notion. He stood up.

'I've riding to do tomorrow. If you'll excuse me.'

The request was formal only. No one ever tried to detain Roche against his wishes.

4

The horse which the livery stable had given him this time was much better than the last. Because he was now marshal and had killed a man? Maybe both. All the same, it felt good to set off on half a day's riding – getting to the Templeton ranch had taken no more than an hour – on a decent mount, most of his worldly possessions in his saddle roll behind him, his old prod spurs on his boots. It was almost like being in front of his old regiment. Too much like. After Bixbee had relieved him he'd gone on to get it wiped out. There'd been just six survivors out of the original enlisted men at the war's end.

All through the morning he'd rarely seen cattle. The land was really too poor but if you acquired enough of it, you'd survive in the long run. Only the Bar Q would make it. He could see the motive of its owners well enough but seeing wasn't approving, or even caring. He only cared about one thing – finding Lucie.

Except that wasn't quite true. He'd be pleased to see Helen again. He'd liked her on the instant, something that hadn't happened to him for a long, long while. He would have made this journey just to see her.

He was two miles off the ranch house, itself hidden by a rise of land that went up to a hundred feet according to the map, though spread out so much the gradient wasn't really noticeable, when he saw the riders coming towards him.

There were four of them, riding towards him at a canter. He kept up his course and speed. There was no point in doing anything else. His horse was tired and couldn't outrun them, nor did he want to.

He checked the sawn-off in the rifle sheath. At close range it would be a far more fearsome weapon than a Colt handgun. His .32 was fully loaded. If it came to it, he had a very slim chance. But the badge on his chest and the fact of William Quinn's invitation would, he guessed, be more useful in the way of allies.

They drew up in line before him. He recognized the two kids he'd seen in the saloon. The two others with them were much more mature, not to say hardbitten. They were all armed with six-shooters, holstered still. He stayed his horse.

'You're on Bar Q land,' the oldest of the party said, a veteran with missing teeth and a cut-down sombrero.

'It's the only way to get to the Bar Q ranch house,' Roche observed mildly.

'You ain't wanted there.'

'Mr William Quinn thought otherwise when he invited me for dinner. You work for the Quinns, don't you.'

'You killed Larry Morton!' one of the boys said, angrily.

Roche wondered if he'd been watching in the dark of the alley, the one who'd reported back. It didn't matter now.

'I kill people who fire pistols at me,' he said coolly, looking still at the grizzled oldster in the truncated sombrero. The unspoken message – control your men or you'll be first to die – got through.

'Calm down, kid.'

'He's the one who—'

'You heard me! I'm ramrodding this outfit and you'll follow orders or you'll be without a job. Understand?'

'Yeah.'

The ramrod looked back to Roche. 'You still ain't welcome on Bar Q land, mister.'

'Mr Quinn says otherwise,' Roche said and left it at that. The time for talking was over. He set his horse moving forward, directly past them.

Nothing happened. They could shoot him in the back but he took them for working cowboys, not gunhands, and he was right. When he got to the top of the rise he saw them still there, watching him, impotently.

He glanced down at the Bar Q ranch house – a large, limewashed 'dobe building more like a Spanish mission than anything but oddly different. He'd expected a big clapboard house in the style that made Lanchester look much like a collection of army hutments but nothing like this, squat, solid and almost fortlike.

'They didn't shoot back there, maybe they won't shoot down there,' he said softly to the horse and set it down the slope at a canter.

At the instance of some obscure inner prompting Roche didn't go to the main door of the great house but went round the back instead. There, everything was normal: a clapboard barn and stables and the usual rickety-looking corral. A Mexican servant took his horse after Roche had taken off his saddle roll and slipped it over his shoulder.

'Take good care of my horse,' he said, 'we've both run risks today.'

'*Sí, señor.*'

He was walking around to the front when he saw Helen come running towards him. She was wearing a yellow gingham dress and her long, lustrous hair was lovely in its simplicity.

'I saw you ride up and then you disappeared!' she said accusingly.

'I saw to my horse first. I admit to being an old cavalryman, ma'am.'

She laughed. 'You should have come straight in. We don't leave horses out in the sun at the Bar Q.'

'My apologies, ma'am.'

She smiled. 'You'll sound foolish calling me "ma'am" while I'm calling you "Philip",' she said.

'Will I, ma'am?'

She suddenly looked stricken. 'I'm sorry, I—'

Roche laughed. 'No, I am … Helen.' He paused, then: 'I was admiring the house as I rode in. I've never quite seen its like.'

'Oh, that's because there *is* nothing like it. It was a ruin when grandfather came out here and started everything.'

'A mission?'

'No, some kind of Indian building.'

'The Apaches?'

She laughed. ' 'Course not. It's Pueblo Indian of some sort, but they'd already moved on. Grandfather patched up the adobe walls and put on a roof and the Bar Q was born.' She paused. 'Come on, I'll show you around. It's cooler inside anyway. The thick adobe walls see to that.'

And keep it warmer at night, Roche thought, but said nothing, allowing himself to be led into the house.

The interior surprised him. The walls

were for the most part plain and white-washed but the few pictures were good quality and the rugs and carpets, a mixture of every kind imaginable, were tastefully arranged. The furniture was Spanish style and heavy but shone from much loving polishing and touched the air with a slight scent of beeswax.

In one of the rooms there was a piano, not the upright kind you got in bars and brothels but an orchestral-style grand.

'Do you play?' he asked as they passed it.

'Not well.'

'I'd like to hear you sometime.'

She smiled. 'Maybe you will. But for now let's find my father.'

They did. He was in one of the side rooms reading a book with a glass of whiskey on the small table beside his leather-upholstered chair. He put the book down, rose and shook Roche by the hand.

'I'm glad you were fortunate, sir. I can only apologize for the fact that one of our hands tried to do you harm.'

'No apology is required, sir. I know it was none of your doing.'

'What are you talking about?' Helen asked.

William Quinn gave his daughter a brief but accurate account of the Morton shooting, stressing the earlier incident in the bar as the cause of it all. Then:

'Am I right, Mr Roche?'

'Perfectly.' Roche didn't have to ask how he knew. It was all over the ranch – with one exception. There had been someone else in that alley. The only question was, who'd sent them? And he knew, almost instinctively, that it wasn't William Quinn. Or his daughter, who'd suddenly gone white.

'He could have killed you!'

'But he didn't.'

Helen looked at him for a long moment then turned and ran off.

Roche watched her go.

'I'm sorry, I seem to have upset her. Did she know Morton well?'

'Well enough to detest him. He was not a pleasant man, but you already know that.'

'So why employ him?'

William Quinn sat down again in his upholstered chair, gestured Roche to one opposite.

'You know perfectly well you don't run a ranch this size with choirboys, Phil – I may call you that?'

'You may and I do, sir.'

Quinn picked up his drink and smiled.

'You also know men who run large businesses don't spend their days reading and drinking whiskey. My brother is the force behind the Bar Q. But you already knew that too. It's hardly a secret.'

'You're well liked, sir.'

'Because no one blames me for anything. I notice you didn't say "well respected" but then I took you for a gentleman on our first meeting. I wasn't wrong. I rarely am.'

Roche considered. He could ask why William Quinn left everything to his brother but it was really none of his concern. Probably because he was weak. And he might be candid enough to admit it too and that would be embarrassing. Worse, it would end the conversation.

'I'll be frank with you, sir. There was a child mentioned in Susan Templeton's will. I was put under an obligation to her. I wish to fulfil it.'

'Naturally,' William Quinn said. He

paused, rubbed his chin. 'That was not the work of the Bar Q, Phil, believe me. My brother can be forceful but he's no killer, despite the stories. And the Templeton ranch would have come to us inevitably, even if Susan had lived. You've been there, I hear. Could a woman alone have made anything of it?'

'No.'

'It truly was Apache work. I can't account for the child but ...' He gestured ineffectually.

Roche felt suddenly cold. William Quinn wasn't lying. He might be wrong or misinformed but he wasn't lying.

'It's a hard country, Phil. I'm not hard enough for it. I know my own weakness.'

'I—'

'There's no need to be polite about the matter. I have my house, my books, my whiskey and above all, my daughter. I count myself an exceptionally fortunate man still.'

Roche nodded, suddenly anxious to turn the conversation.

'What's the book, sir?'

'A volume of Gibbon. I was reading about Bohemund, a crusader who was the son of a Norman pirate. Do you recall the tale?'

'No, sir. I've read parts but there are just too many emperors for me.'

'Bohemund was only a second son but for all that he founded a principality and married the daughter of the King of France.'

'And?'

Quinn smiled. 'He came to a more or less bad end. Everybody did. That's why it's the "decline and fall". Ah, I see my daughter's coming back to claim you, Phil. Her conversation will be more cheery. She only reads books which have a happy ending.'

Roche stood up.

'Pay no attention to me, Phil. I'm just a foolish, fortunate man.' He paused. 'I'll see you at dinner.'

'I'll look forward to it, sir.'

Helen led him wordlessly out on to the porch – a wooden addition to the original building, whitewashed to fit in.

'I'm sorry I reacted so badly,' she said at last.

Roche smiled. 'I didn't think of it that way at all. People should react against killing.'

'Were you in danger?'

'Some, but it wasn't the first time.'

'The war?'

'And after.'

'I'm sorry.'

Roche found himself wanting to tell her everything, including the parentage of Lucie. He felt an enormous sympathy with her – maybe that wasn't quite the right word but he couldn't explain it further. Not here, not now. He glanced out across the land, more brown than green, all harshly delineated in the stark sunlight.

'I went to school in the state capital,' Helen said suddenly, 'but I couldn't wait to get back here. Some people think it's a cruel desert place but it's my home. I love it.'

'I've seen many places,' Roche said slowly, 'but it's the people who live there that truly count. Some places are more beautiful than others, richer or poorer, arid or lush, but in the end a place is just … a place.'

She smiled at him as if about to say something important, but didn't. Eventually she said:

'Dinner's at six.'

Then she disappeared.

Compared to the scale of the house the dining-room was of relatively modest dimensions. The table seated eight though only three places were set. William Quinn sat at the head and the other two near him, facing each other, an arrangement Roche found not unpleasant. The image of Helen coming to dine in a pale dress that took gold from the candlelight, her face like a jewel itself, was something to remember. William Quinn himself broke the spell.

'I believe I have a further apology to make. It seems some Bar Q men braced you on your way here.'

'I prefer to think of it as greeting me,' Roche said, only lightly sardonic.

'You are most kind.'

Roche looked to Helen. This time she hadn't reacted at all. She had known what her father was about to say.

They made small talk as the courses were brought in by Mexican servants – a fine soup, then a T-bone steak, a sweet pudding concocted of cornflour and fruit which Roche didn't know the name of but which he enjoyed nevertheless. Then, cheese and biscuits, and lastly coffee. He noticed that Helen eschewed the former. He didn't. For all this was cow country there was little in the way of cheese-making and he enjoyed a good cheese.

'Shall we retire to the smoking-room, Phil?'

'By all means.'

'You don't object if Helen comes with us?'

'By no means. I thought she was too perfect ... but I'm broad-minded. I'll even light the cigar for her.'

Helen laughed. 'I don't mind the smell, I even quite enjoy it – at a distance.'

'My apologies, ma'am,' Roche said, making a slight bow and smiling back at her.

'Accepted,' she said skippingly, then took her father's arm as they left the remains of the dinner for the servants to clear away.

'There's the brandy – help yourself,' William Quinn said, as they settled in the smoking-room. 'I'll stick to whiskey.'

Roche nodded but didn't pour himself a drink. He drank only sparingly and despite the idyllic elements of the evening, he was working still.

'Let me light that for you,' Helen said as he clipped the end off one of her father's Havanas. He watched her walk to the fire and light a spill, then let her set the flame to his cigar. She concentrated on the job in hand but Roche looked at her face. Perhaps Susan had been conventionally prettier but Helen had a loveliness all of her own.

'You'll forgive me if I talk business,' Quinn said.

'Of course.'

'It's about the Templeton ranch – your ranch. The Bar Q is interested in it. An offer has been made.'

'Mr Andrews mentioned it.'

'I'll raise it to five thousand dollars.'

Roche drew on his cigar. It was excellent.

'It's a very fair offer,' he acknowledged.

'And?'

'I'm not interested in selling at the moment, sir. I'm not a poor man but even if I were, the will put me under an obligation. A matter of honour.'

'Lucie?'

Roche nodded.

83

'It's hopeless, I'm afraid.'

'I still have to try.'

'Of course, I understand that. There's also the matter of the remuda and the stock—'

'I'd be obliged if you'd continue the present arrangement. I'm in no position to care for either at the moment.'

'That's fine. I'm glad you trust me.'

'I trust you, sir.'

Quinn smiled, then turned to his daughter.

'He didn't include you in that, my dear, but take it rather as a compliment. You're too pretty to be trusted entirely.'

'Not at all,' Roche said, joining in the banter and glad the 'business' was over, 'I trust Helen implicitly.'

And found he meant every word. It must have come over that way too for Helen said nothing, tried to look demure but managed flustered instead.

'You're staying in this country, Phil?'

'I hadn't thought, sir.'

'You've no ties back East?'

'I've no ties anywhere.'

'This is good country if you know how to handle it—'

'But maybe our guest doesn't know that; not everyone does.'

Roche looked up and saw the newcomer. There was no need to ask who he was. He and William could almost have been twins but where William was gentle, Harry was forceful, exuding power. He strode over and shook Roche – who had risen – by the hand.

'Sorry I missed dinner. Some cattle had wandered into a draw – but you don't really want the details now, do you?' he paused. 'Will you drink with me?'

'A brandy.'

Harry Quinn poured two glasses, handed him one.

'It's Mexican, not French. William here won't touch it but I go with my own prejudices.'

Roche sipped it. It was good. He said as much.

Harry Quinn poured himself another.

'Cows are stupid animals, Mr Roche. Looking after them's thirsty work.' He glanced at his brother. 'Has he agreed?'

'He hasn't disagreed,' William Quinn said mildly.

'Eh?'

'Mr Roche feels himself under an obligation to the late Mrs Templeton. To find
Lucie.'

Harry Quinn looked straight at Roche.
'Do you think we didn't look? My men
spent days looking. Go and ask them. We
just couldn't find her.'

'It was as if the Hidden Apaches had
taken her,' Helen said.

'Who are they?' Roche asked quickly.

Harry Quinn snorted. 'The local equiva-
lent of the fairies, the Little People.'

Roche looked to Helen. She nodded.

'I'm sorry. I shouldn't have interrupted.'

'You didn't,' Roche said.

'Whatever, Apaches did take her. Real
ones, a party of raiding Mimbreños. I hear
tell young James at the fort is about to
deal with them. We thought they were in
Mexico but they've been hiding up in the
Broken Hills all along.'

'When did you hear this, sir?'

'Today. He's still at the fort.'

'I'll ride there tomorrow.'

'And the Templeton ranch?'

'Afterwards.'

Harry Quinn poured himself a third
glass of brandy.

'As you will, but you're wasting your time. Even with a boy child the chances would be a hundred to one against. Small raiding parties don't keep prisoners.'

'So why did they take her?'

'Do you know Apaches?'

'No.'

'Neither does anyone else. But you learn to fear them. They lived on this land before we came and the Pueblos and Spaniards feared them. The land's cruel but they were more cruel. When the Sioux and the Cheyenne raided in Apache lands, few went home. The Mexicans pay a bounty for their scalps as if they were wolves and they hate them worse. Believe me, they took her with them aways and then they cut her throat.'

'I need to find her, Mr Quinn. Guessing isn't enough.' It was a mild enough contradiction but Harry Quinn froze. Out of the corner of his eye Roche noticed how worried William Quinn looked. His brother wasn't used to being contradicted. Ever.

And then the moment passed. Harry Quinn laughed.

'You're right, Mr Roche, it's a good guess

but just a guess after all. A matter of honour can't be settled by a mere guess.' He paused. 'Is that your horse in the stable?'

'The livery's.'

'I'll have the pick of our remuda saddled for you and I'll return the nag. After you've been to the fort, I'd be obliged if you'd see me. We may be able to talk business then.'

'We may indeed, sir.'

Quinn poured himself a fourth brandy and left, quite unaffected by the alcohol. Roche couldn't help noticing the way Helen looked at him as he went – with almost daughterly affection.

Roche found that displeased him greatly.

5

The horse was splendid and had been waiting for him just as Harry Quinn had promised. Roche had wondered whether it was part of a scheme to call him a horse-thief but had quickly rejected the idea. It would be too crude and besides, he still had hope of buying the ranch. It was a courtesy and a clever one. He had to return the horse and give Harry Quinn a second chance at persuading him.

Helen had been up to see him go but they had been oddly formal. In the candle-light of the night before he had felt a certain rapport, almost an intimacy, but with the daylight it was almost as if they were passing strangers.

No one had offered directions to the fort and he hadn't asked. He'd seen the map and his old facility was all he needed. A brisk twenty-five-mile ride over unbroken country and he'd be there.

He kept a good pace. The horse was up to it and he wanted to be on time. It was a harsh, dry, hot land but he found himself getting to appreciate it: the sudden patches of green, the saguaro cacti, the stunted bushes and in the distance before him the grey and yellow mountains.

The sun was getting high by the time he arrived at Fort Bixbee. It wasn't much of a fort but it had obviously been built as a fort, probably by the Spaniards a century or more before, at least well before the Spanish–American War. Unconsciously he'd been half-expecting a stockade of logs but there were no trees locally; all that was available was mud brick, if you could find water enough to make them. Very suitable for Fort Bixbee after all.

The sentry at the gate let him in for the price of his name.

'Go to the orderly office, sir.'

Roche did so. A corporal in the anteroom

asked him to wait, rapped on a nameless door. A few moments later he was inside shaking hands with Lieutenant James.

'I wasn't sure you'd really come,' James said, 'and truth to tell you've picked an awkward time. We're about to go hunting.'

'I've come to join the party,' Roche said and explained, saying as much as he had at the Bar Q but no more.

'Quinn's probably right,' Jams said when he'd finished. 'You can always asks Sergeant Dobbs though, he's an old hand here.'

'He's coming with us?' Roche asked, assuming permission to make it harder to refuse.

James smiled. That kind of artfulness wasn't new to him.

'No, Dobbs stays. He's busted his foot. I was going to leave him to command the fort and take my only other commissioned officer along and damn standing orders, but if you're willing to accept the tempo-rary rank of civilian scout I can save my career.'

Roche laughed.

'You accept?'

'Why not? I'm already an unpaid

marshal, why not become an unpaid scout as well?'

'Who said anything about "unpaid"?'

'Me, just now. Best not to put my name on paper. The United States Army and I aren't on the best of terms.'

'Oh, that. I doubt the army cares any more. Bixbee never got his second star and he's retired now anyway. According to Dobbs you were winning too many battles independently and so Bixbee relieved you on a technicality.'

'Dobbs served under me?'

'Not in your regiment but in your brigade. He speaks highly of you.'

'And less so of Bixbee.' Roche suddenly found the anger he'd been carrying around about the circumstances of his dismissal had all drained away. He said: 'As divisional commander Bixbee was under enormous pressure to gain a quick victory. He picked the wrong place. I said so loudly. You know the result.'

'Yeah, he lost half his command, a classic Pyrrhic victory but still capable of being called a triumph in the newspapers. That's why they kept him on as a general after the war but didn't let him rise.'

'I was the boy who'd cried wolf and wolf there'd been. The army has its ways to deal with people like that. I was put on boards of inquiry on the quartermaster side, investigating the supply of oats, bridles and the like until the war ended and I could be quietly discharged.'

'I'm sorry.'

'So was I, but come to think about it, I'd probably be dead otherwise. Boards of inquiry are pretty safe berths.'

'I can't say as much for our little expedition.'

'How little?'

'Two thirds of my entire command, twenty-two men.'

Roche shook his head. The army really had cut back.

'How many does Carlito have?'

'Seven, including himself.'

'Good odds.'

'Not according to Dobbs. But you can bring my men back if I can't.'

'The army wouldn't approve of that.'

'I'd be beyond caring,' James said sensibly. Then: 'If she's alive, we'll get Lucie back. She's yours, isn't she?'

'How did you know?'

'The way you said her name.'

Roche sighed. If he was that obvious, maybe Harry Quinn knew. And Helen. That would explain why she'd been so distant when he'd left.

'Judge for yourself,' he said and showed James the letter. James read it slowly, then handed it back.

'Obviously I didn't know her but I'd say she makes herself pretty plain.'

Roche found that he needed neither to defend Susan nor to condemn her. He'd half-hated and half-loved her for years – why else had he come West? – and now ... nothing. All he cared about was Lucie. And Helen. But it was the kid who needed him now.

James seemed to understand his silence, nodded.

'I've forms to fill so why don't you seek out Dobbs? We'll talk over dinner. You can stow your gear in my room. There's a spare bunk.'

'Surely,' Roche said. He was under orders again. James might be just a first lieutenant but he was also the man in command and that was all that mattered.

Roche checked his girth and then mounted up but waited for the soldiers to ride out of the fort. They were mostly very young men and they didn't ride quite like cavalrymen. At last it was his turn to tack on to the party. As a civilian, scout or not, he had no place in a military ceremony.

At least there were no weeping wives to see the half-troop off. In fact there were no women on the post and not too many men either now. Just Second Lieutenant Kesay standing formally by the gate and Dobbs propped up beside him on crutches representing the corporal's guard that was being left.

Roche touched his hat as he passed them, then urged on his horse to join the head of the small column, noticing the Springfield rifles of the troopers as he passed. One-shot weapons. The few non-coms had Colt pistols but if the Indians had Henry or Winchester repeating carbines ...

James was pleased to see him.

'You were welcome at the head of the column.'

'I would have felt I was out of uniform. Want me to take the point?'

James shook his head. 'I'll let one of my men do that, later. But I could use your advice.'

Which was probably out of date. Roche didn't underrate himself as a soldier but he just didn't know Apaches. Even the 'expert', Sergeant Dobbs, whom he'd spoken to the day before, had admitted he didn't really know them either: he'd chased them enough but never caught up with them, just their gory handiwork.

'I'm not sure I have any to offer,' Roche said.

'Then you really are the exception,' James said. 'Everyone else has been brimming with it for days.'

'I know the feeling,' Roche said. 'But advice is easy. Being in command isn't.'

James just nodded, then: 'You never know, Carlito and his band might just decide to surrender.'

'It's safest to assume they won't, though I admit it's possible. If they're short of horses, food and ammunition and know they've been spotted ...' He stopped, intentionally.

'What is it?'

'It was something Dobbs said. Apaches

aren't usually spotted. Or if they are, those who do the spotting get their throats cut ...'

'I'm listening.'

'I'm thinking the easiest way of getting horses and food and ammunition is by letting it come to you.'

'You mean, take it from us?'

'Why not? Assume they know everything about your command. They see without being seen so it's likely enough. That means above all that they know your strength.'

'It's still three to one."

'Maybe they expected a smaller patrol. In which case, with the odds now against them, we don't see 'em. But we could do something about those odds.'

'You mean, split my forces in the presence of the enemy?' James protested. 'I could lose half my men.'

'Only if you risked half,' Roche said and went on to explain as the column of men and horses moved north, towards the Broken Hills.

The Broken Hills, in reality a full-blown mountain range, were visible now in the distance, rising like black and much separated teeth out of brown and green foothills. A ridge ran parallel to them and on the reverse slope of this the column waited, only James and Roche lying atop it looking out at their eventual destination.

Between the ridge and the foothills was a valley spotted with saguaro cacti and the occasional stunted bush through which the trail north wended its way. No river ran in this valley though floodwater must have cut it and washed it smooth long ago.

Roche had seen the army map on the eve of departure and James had discussed his plans over it. He intended to make his first camp at Pueblo Viejo – a long-abandoned Pueblo Indian village three miles along the valley trail.

'There,' Roche said, pointing it out now, 'that's where I'd attack a small party if I wanted their horses. What's more predictable than that a small party would check it on their way in as they went into the Broken Hills themselves?'

'Still, they could be twenty miles off yet,' James said dubiously.

'Only if they intend to hide, and then we'll never find them. No, my bet is they'll have a man watching this ridge now, ready to run back and report.'

'Why the village?'

Roche knew the West Pointer was just trying to think of objections because he had been taught to think that way. Fundamentally, he was convinced. Roche said patiently:

'We're assuming they're afoot so they'll need the patrol stopped and they'll need cover. They'll also know how we operate, that we have to check it out. I'd guess Carlito thought of it as the site of a potential trap from the beginning. But a trap like that can close on him as well as us. Let's force his hand.'

'It's a fair ride, getting on for four miles, I'd say.'

'I'd say a bit less,' Roche said and then stopped himself from going on, sensing that it wasn't needed, that James was already sold.

James had been putting off the final decision but Roche's clever tactical reading and above all the sight of the Broken Hills themselves decided him. Desperate men could hole up there for ever and Apaches were that to begin with; pushed, they'd eat their remaining horses and even their moccasins if need arose.

'Pick your men,' James said.

Roche shook his head. He was no longer a commissioned officer even if he were about to act the part. He couldn't choose men for likely death.

'Very well, you can have the last two pairs,' James said and went back down the slope, Roche following him.

The rest was checking of canteens, selecting the pack horses they would take with them, for a patrol without pack-horses would look too much like a gambit. James made sure they all had handguns, though as they were all recruits, enlisted on the same day, James picked the eldest for senior soldier and instructed him to obey the scout implicitly. It was an illegal order – Roche wasn't in the line of command – but the recruit didn't dispute it, nor ever would. If everything succeeded, he'd be a hero; if not, incapable of complaint. Besides which, the soldier was more than anxious to have someone to give him orders.

'You can have my Colt,' James told Roche, reaching for it.

'Thanks, but no,' Roche said. 'That's a sawn-off in my saddle sheath and for close up I'm better off with my .32.'

'No stopping power.'

'It has if you hit where you're aiming.'

'So, good luck – and I hope you find the girl.'

'Thanks,' Roche said as they shook hands. He then turned to the senior soldier. 'What's your name, son?'

'Brown, sir.'

'Just follow me then, Brown. The rest of you follow him, single file.' He mounted and watched the four soldiers do likewise, then led them slowly over the rise and down into the valley. There had been no point in arranging a signal for James and the rest to come after them. They would simply ride towards the sound of gunfire.

They rode down the centre of the high valley. After a while, Roche had them dismount and walk their horses. Everything had to look ordinary when you were headed for the jaws of a trap.

Were they? It was always the same in war. You made plans, assumptions, guesses. Sometimes they worked out, sometimes not. Carlito might always prefer to sucker them further in, into the heart of the mountains. But then, how could he know that they'd oblige, that they wouldn't stop at the foothills? And they were temptingly weak.

Roche assumed Carlito was watching them now, looking at them through the eyes of need. Without horses they could stay and starve in the mountains but everywhere else they were vulnerable. Yet with horses they could ride and raid right down into Mexico and something like safety.

James thought of Carlito as a savage, a cruel fool. Roche simply thought of him as the enemy and it was better to overestimate an enemy than not. When, after they'd dined frugally in the mess the last night in the fort and James had spread out the map and proposed spending the second night out at the abandoned pueblo, Roche had suddenly understood. This was Carlito's trap. He had felt it with a certainty, though for all that he'd kept his own counsel. James would have resented advice then. On the trail it could be given in private and casually, that much easier to accept. This was not only James's first command, it was his first campaign, and he'd fight against having it usurped in any obvious way. Besides, when Roche had seen Pueblo Viejo in the distant, muddy flesh, something else had clicked: he had known just *why* it had been set there.

'Hey, Mr Roche, do you reckon they'll really come?' Brown asked.

'They'll come,' Roche said, committing himself. 'Never doubt that. Now, let's mount up again.'

What had been a mark on a map and then a pattern in the distance was now assembling itself into a small adobe village – oddly square, a grid of small houses. Another half an hour at the walk and they would be there. Would Carlito be in place, hidden with his men, waiting? Despite everything, for nothing is certain in war, it could still turn out to be just another fruitless patrol, a walk and a ride in the afternoon sun with nothing to show for it but sweat and dust.

If it weren't for Lucie he'd be hoping it

was so. He could already feel the fear like a weight in his belly and the four recruits would be the same. He'd felt it the first time too, and every time since.

'Whatever happens, stay together.'

They'd try, he knew. It was the obvious way to survive. But whether they'd succeed was another matter.

The attack when it came was, as always, unexpected. They were about a hundred yards from the village when the two shots rang out and one of the soldiers screamed. But the firing had come from behind them!

Roche turned, saw two Apaches rising up from the ground, casting off blankets and showering dust and dirt all around them. They had obviously been lying in slit trenches. Maybe they'd even ridden over them. Roche grabbed the sawn-off from its sheath and fired. One of them went down. Roche almost cried out – *Into the pueblo* ... And stopped himself. It was too obvious.

'Make for the bluff.' He spurted his horse, hoping the rest would follow. He caught sight of Brown riding beside him, a revolver in one hand, the reins in the other.

'Got to make a stand—'

He broke off suddenly. It was as if a sledgehammer had hit his head. Then there was blood in his eyes, obscuring his vision, but he still spurred forward. With the bluff behind them they could defend themselves. Carlito had intended to drive them into the village for cover but they'd have died there and in very short order.

He wiped the blood out of his eyes, saw the bluff sheer up in front of him, slipped from his horse, letting go of the reins, knowing he should have held on to them. There were blue shirts beside him but although the blood was no longer running into his eyes he could tell no more than that; his eyes weren't focusing properly.

Guns were being fired, revolvers – his men – and he knew the horses were lost. They were recruits, no more. Hell, he'd done the same. He fired the other barrel of his sawn-off, thought he heard someone scream but wasn't sure. He tried to draw his .32 for what use it might be in this wild fight but oddly the effort was beyond him; then he found himself falling, blinded again by blood.

His last conscious thought was that he would have liked to see Lucie, if only just once. And then the pain hit him; the noise of battle faded and the light with it.

'I'll take out Blackie,' Helen told the stable boy.

'*Sí, señorita*,' came the reply and he disappeared into the gloom of the stables.

Helen Quinn walked to the front of the house, looking out over the land. Usually the view pleased her but not now – it was too dry, almost lifeless. As if there was something missing. Philip Roche. Even his unspoken name had power over her.

Damn him, she thought, couldn't she get him out of her mind? But she couldn't. She hadn't been able to since their first meeting.

It was a new feeling and it both exhausted and annoyed her. She wasn't sure she wanted to feel that way about anybody yet, but that was purely academic. She did.

Uncle Harry was standing by the porch, smoking one of his cheap black cigars. Her father would only have the best but Harry Quinn wasn't so particular. He didn't need to be, she thought; he already had the ranch and everything.

'Going riding?' he asked, a little mockingly. Because she was dressed for the part – riding-skirt and jacket and a little riding-hat she'd had sent from St Louis. A waste of time really when no one saw it but the hands – and Uncle Harry.

'I'm giving Blackie a ride.'

Harry Quinn laughed. He didn't dress to ride; he didn't ride to give his favourite horse a work-out. Had he a favourite horse? She doubted it. A good, fresh horse was all he demanded to do his work running the Bar Q. Which her father wouldn't do....

'You look annoyed,' Quinn said.

She probably did but she didn't admit it. She didn't admit anything.

'If it's that Roche feller, don't get your hopes up. He'll be back but it'll be for once only. He's no rancher. He'll sell and then he'll be gone. I know the type – fancy clothes and manners but no good.'

She looked at him. 'You're wrong.'

Harry Quinn shrugged. 'Maybe I am,

but not about him being no rancher. That's obvious. And he's no fool either. He'll take the money I offer him.'

'How much money?'

'I'll go up to eight thousand, though don't tell him that. I'm hoping to buy him out for six.'

'Is the Templeton ranch worth that much?'

He drew on his cigar, then: 'Not in itself. But it would take us that much nearer town. One of these days there'll be a spur line to Lanchester. I want us to be able to run cattle straight into town over our own land when that happens.'

Did he want that enough to… She broke off the disloyal thought. Harry Quinn had his faults but it was inconceivable that a tenth of what the town gossip credited him with was true. It was precisely that, gossip. The small ranchers whose land the Bar Q had swallowed up had come to be swallowed up precisely because they *were* that, small. This was big, arid country. You needed to think big to survive. Uncle Harry always thought big.

'You didn't like him, did you?' she asked, not quite sure why.

'No, not much. He's a killer with the manners of a gentleman, girl. Don't let him fool you.'

'It wasn't his fault. Morton—'

'Forget Morton! He wasn't the first by any manner of means. I made a few enquiries of my own. He'd already killed four men I know about before he arrived here.'

'He's wanted?' Helen asked, noticing the tremble in her voice and quite unable to do anything about it.

'No, everyone of 'em legal. He was a gambler on the riverboats. No charges were ever laid but they never are, there.' He paused. 'Don't be fooled by his fancy ways. He's not for you.'

Her stomach felt tight. She knew Uncle Harry wasn't lying. It wasn't his way, though he was good at selecting the 'truth' he wanted you to believe. But what really upset her was the fact that it didn't make any difference what Philip Roche had done before. It didn't alter the way she felt about him. It should, but it didn't.

'I doubt whether he's interested in me anyway,' she forced herself to say, hoping it was a lie even as she said it.

'Everyone's interested in the Bar Q, girl,' Harry Quinn said. 'Anyway, I reckon he'll be out chasing Carlito now. Maybe that savage will solve all our problems.'

Helen went cold. Harry Quinn was notable for his tactlessness but that was beyond the bounds – so far beyond that she didn't know how to reply. Then she saw the stable boy leading Blackie to her; the great, sleek animal caught sight of her too and pulled on the reins to get to her.

'Ride safely,' Uncle Harry said and turned to go back into the house.

Helen did ride safely and slowly until she was out of sight of the house – her father often watched her ride from the window of his room – but then she tore off the foolish St Louis bonnet and let the stallion have his head. She felt the wind of their own making tousle her hair and brush her cheek and cool the tears running down them. Whether they were of rage at Uncle Harry for what he'd said or for fear that she might lose Philip Roche – and he was hardly hers to lose yet – to Carlito, she didn't know. But the pounding hoofs and speed of the great, black horse made both her rage and her uncertainty a little easier to bear.

6

'How do you feel, Phil?'

'Amazed to feel anything at all,' Roche said, looking up at the still-indistinct blue figure. 'I thought—'

'A ball creased your head.' James paused. 'I saw it all through my binoculars. The pair of them just rose up out of the ground. Amazing. They were trying to drive you into the pueblo. The rest of them were waiting there, ten of them. There were more than we thought.' He paused. 'If you'd gone in …'

'The horses,' Roche said, woozily, 'I lost the horses …'

'That really saved you. They were more

interested in getting the horses than in killing you.'

Roche suddenly came to full consciousness. 'The others...?'

'Brown's wounded in the arm but he'll make it. He'll also make corporal in very short order. He more or less held them off single handed until we arrived. But the rest didn't make it.'

Roche sighed. 'If—'

'My decision, Phil. Besides, if we'd done it as I originally intended we could all have died. It was a very neat trap indeed.' He paused, then: 'We found their wicki-ups. Two of 'em on the other side of the bluff. No sign of your girl. I'm sorry.'

'Can I talk to the prisoners?'

'Only one had any English. He didn't know anything about a white girl. I believed him. We asked pretty forcefully. But he's dead now. Carlito's alive but he doesn't speak English.'

'He might speak some Spanish. I think I've a few rags of that left. Help me to my feet.'

James did and for a moment Roche stood uncertainly, the world threatening to spin about him. The pueblo was about eighty yards off, soldiers moving around and in it. And just to his right were three bodies in blue, hats over their faces.

'I want to see Carlito.'

'OK, I'll give you a hand.'

'I can walk. Where's my gun, the sawn-off…?'

James pointed it out with the toe of his boot. A bullet had caught it, smashing the trigger.

'Probably saved your life. Want it as a memento?' he made to pick it up.

'Hell, I'm not that sentimental,' Roche said. 'I just need to speak to Carlito.'

James shrugged, took his arm. 'Let's go and try it.'

All through the war Roche had never had even the slightest of wounds. He'd seen men die all around him but he'd been immune and now, after this bitter little skirmish with savage Apaches, he was being led like a child. But he didn't reject the helping hand. The dizziness was fading but his legs felt still as if they were made of rubber.

Troopers were carrying Apache corpses into one of the houses, Roche saw when they got to the pueblo. Their eventual tomb, he supposed.

'Have they been searched?'

'Yes. Nothing. They'd only four rifles between them and few enough cartridges. Their food supplies were low too – three days' supply of jerky. They needed us to come here unsuspecting.'

'They fought well.'

'They killed three of my men,' James said with finality.

Carlito was in the tiny plaza at the pueblo's centre, kneeling, his hands and feet tied. There was blood on his head too but from a blow rather than a bullet; otherwise he was uninjured.

He was a small man, wiry, his red shirt and white Mexican-style trousers engrained with dirt and now splotched with blood, but he had an air of quiet dignity about him, even in defeat.

Roche went and stood before him.

'Carlito!'

The Apache looked up.

'*Busco a mi hija*,' Roche said, furiously trying to recall the bit of Spanish he'd learnt in his youth on a visit to Vera Cruz.

Carlito said nothing but from the look in

his eyes Roche knew he had understood:
I'm looking for my daughter. But that was
too vague a question. He tried to frame
the Spanish phrase he wanted but the
words would scarcely come.

'*Una niña. Pequeña. Cinco años.*'

Still Carlito just looked at him.

'*El rancho* Templeton. *Nel sud. Hace un
mes.*' The Templeton ranch, in the south, a
month ago.

'*No comprendo.*' Carlito spoke slowly, his
Spanish as halting as Roche's own.

'*Ustedes mataron a su madre. Hace un
mes. Un ataque. Nel sud.*' Your hand killed
her mother a month ago, in the south.

'*No eramos en el sud. Eramos aquí,
esperando los soldados.*'

'What did he say?' James asked.

'That he never raided in the south or
anywhere. They were here waiting for
you.'

'He's probably lying. If you want him
persuaded—'

'No,' Roche said. He believed the
Apache. If they'd raided south, why just
one ranch and a poor one at that? A lone
Apache? That too was barely conceivable;
Carlito had fought too well, he was a

clever enemy, far too clever to divide his forces for no gain. No, they had been waiting for a patrol and its horses. A good plan. It might have worked if James had been left to his own devices. Roche turned away.

'*Señor.*'

Roche turned about.

'*Tiene que busca a la niña en los alogiamientos de los Apaches Ocultados.*'

'*En donde?*'

But Carlito merely stared at the ground, and somehow Roche knew that not all the rifle butts in the troop would get another word out of him.

'Well?'

'He said to look for the girl with the Hidden Apaches.'

'He didn't say where they were?'

'No.'

'I reckon not.'

Roche tried to clear his head. Hadn't Helen said something about the Hidden Apaches too? He looked to James.

The fort commander shook his head.

'It's their old lost Indian myth,' he said. 'There's the White Mountain Apaches, the Mimbreños, et cetera, et cetera, and

118

finally los Apaches Ocultados, the Hidden Apaches. Doc Fletcher told me of them back at the fort.' He paused. 'I reckon it's just a cruel way of saying "with the dead". Speaking of Doc Fletcher, you want to let him see your head when we get back.'

It was then that Roche noticed the soldiers working on the roof of the house opposite. They'd rigged up a pole – taken from the roof of the house – and got it to jut out over the plaza like a barber's pole. Why? He recalled that Carlito had kept glancing in that direction as they'd talked. Suddenly he turned to James.

'You're not—'

'Don't argue, Phil. We crossed the state line yesterday afternoon. This is Federal Territory. Carlito was taken in arms against the United States. I'm going to hang him.'

'Don't do it,' Roche said simply.

'And send him back to the reservation, from which they'll break out again and raid here or south into Mexico and kill women and kids? I'd have hanged 'em all if any but him had survived.'

Roche saw it was useless to argue. James was set on it and he had all the

119

power here. And hanging Carlito would do his career no harm at all, either. A successful skirmish was in itself small beer but being known as the man who'd caught and hanged the mighty Carlito – whoever he was – would make First Lieutenant James into a coming man. A captaincy in short order and a brevet majority soon after. He might well end up a chicken colonel or maybe even a brigadier general. Just like Bixbee.

Two soldiers pulled Carlito to his feet and dragged him across to the house. A rope was thrown over the pole and tied unceremoniously around the Apache's neck. (The usual thirteen turns were not for Indians.) One of the soldiers loosed the bindings on his legs.

'*Ha luchado bien*,' Roche called out to him.

Carlito looked at him, almost nodded.

Then James gave the word and the Apache war leader was hoisted off the ground. He started kicking immediately. Roche turned away. He had seen hangings enough. So, oddly, did James.

'What did you say to him?'

'Just that he fought well. At least, that's

what I intended to say. It's not my day for translating.'

'It sounded good to me.' He paused. 'I'm sorry if you disapprove but he'd have done much worse to us if he'd won.'

Roche couldn't gainsay that. And then it struck him that Carlito had watched the makeshift gallows being erected as they'd talked. He'd known he'd nothing either to gain or lose by talking. And Apaches didn't lie. He *hadn't* lied.

In one swift motion Roche drew his hitherto unused .32, turned and fired three times at the swinging and kicking form. It swung still but the kicking ceased. Roche reholstered the gun and turned to James.

'You don't object?'

'What good would it do if I did? Besides, that's a common courtesy out here in the West, I believe.'

'I suppose it is,' Roche said, glad that James had assumed he knew the reason for it already. He didn't. It was a very special courtesy to a man who'd just told him Lucie was alive.

Roche spent only two days at Fort Bixbee.

He suspected Lieutenant James was finally pleased to see the back of him. Two heroes were one too many and besides, he didn't feel like one. Better to leave the stage to one who did.

James had even given him a parting present – one of the four rifles taken from the starveling Indians, an old, converted flintlock of the sort given to reservation Indians for hunting. It was heavy and accurate and appallingly slow to reload. He wasn't sure he really wanted a memento but his rifle sheath was empty and so there it stayed. Of more value was an army map of the region. James had been less pleased to provide that – they had to be accounted for, unlike junk guns, but he hadn't been able to bring himself to refuse. Roche had made his career and he knew it. Hanging Carlito had just been the icing on the cake ... and could even go mouldy. Roche rather hoped it would, though he doubted it.

He nooned on Madison's Butte – an extravagant name for an otherwise unmemorable hill, probably named in drink – and ate bread and cheese while studying the map.

Thankfully, no one at the fort had asked him about Lucie or los Apaches Ocultados. Doc Fletcher had confined his enquiries to whether his head still hurt. It didn't, so he had prescribed a shot of whiskey, a medicine he had great faith in for he seemed to consume a bottle a day without any obvious effect. Sergeant Dobbs had been more interested in the 'Battle of Pueblo Viejo' as James now called it, a somewhat overblown description though doubtless it would catch on. Dobbs guessed how it had been but Roche took care not to dispute the official version. Let James have the glory; as a serving officer it was of some use to him. For a man looking for his daughter, it was a pure distraction. The question of the Hidden Apaches wasn't, but if he'd had to justify his ideas on the subject it would have made the whole business seem even more of a long shot.

For it amounted to a single idea. Where could you hide a tribe of Apaches? Among other, more peaceful Indians? But the Pueblo Indians and their like hated Apaches – the word itself meant 'enemy' – so that failed. The alternative was that the name itself was misleading, that the

Indians weren't so much hidden as living in a 'hidden' place – Las Sierras Ocultados, for instance. There were Indians in all the hills but no one paid too much attention to them so long as they caused no trouble.

In fact, all that made the Apache distinct was their raiding and fighting. (Their language was hardly to the point. One Indian language sounded much like another, all incomprehensible. You communicated with them in Spanish, broken English or by gesture.) So a tribe that neither raided nor fought just weren't Apaches. All he needed was a location.

It was a brilliant idea and Roche was almost proud of it. But there was a serious drawback – it wasn't on the map.

Roche didn't despair. Obviously they were *hidden* hills, after all, and the place to hide hills on a map was under another name.

The map names danced before his eyes. He had the feeling it should be obvious but that didn't help. He washed down the last of his portion of cheese with tepid water from his canteen, stowed away the map. He'd better get his horse back to the Bar Q. At least he'd see Helen and …

And suddenly he knew! He could also guess who'd killed Susan, and maybe why. It all fitted. He unscrewed his canteen again, wetted his kerchief and moistened the nose of his horse.

'There'll be water by evening, jughead,' he said, 'but a hard ride before that.' The horse nuzzled his hand.

He didn't need to get the map out again. He knew the direction – due east.

7

It was two hours after noon when he came to the foothills. To the south, half a day's riding, the Bar Q was a white spot on the horizon. These were the low, nameless mountains he had seen from there, looking north.

He rode until he came to the pass. It too had no name on the map, nothing save a number of parallel contour lines pointing north. It was in that direction that he angled his weary horse.

He reckoned he would find what he was looking for on the reverse slope of the first line of rocky hills, if there was anything to find at all and it wasn't a mere figment of his imagination.

He was tired. His head still ached a little and his legs were raw. He'd done more riding in the last week than he had in years. He stopped once to let his horse drink at a rill and filled his canteen too.

The pass narrowed after that and the ground began to rise up. Ahead was something like a natural gateway, not on the map, which gave him to doubting that anything the map said of the interior of the hills would be correct. They'd mapped the outlines and measured the heights from a distance and made assumptions. Army cartographers weren't supposed to do that but given the amount of country to be mapped they sometimes abridged the procedure. It didn't usually matter. It...

He saw the rifle glinting and heard the shot a second later. The bullet plucked at the sleeve of his coat. His mind calculated automatically: 150 yards off, fifty feet high. A good shot from a Winchester carbine. The second bullet confirmed the guess, following in just the time it took to work the lever action of a Winchester and aim quickly, but by then he was off his horse, grabbing his rifle as he went, and running back down the pass itself. It missed by yards. The sniper had wasted his first, carefully aimed shot.

He ran across the pass, ducking and weaving. He wasn't exactly thinking, just reacting. Another bullet smashed into a clump of rocks a yard in front of him but he made it to the shelter of those same rocks before the next came, short this time.

Only then did he think of the rifle in his hands – the junk rifle. But it was all he had. The ammunition was in an old kerchief tied around the upper stock and he ripped it free – four paper cartridges and just three caps. Three shots.

Charging a muzzle loader while lying on the ground was something Roche had never tried before. It was awkward. He pulled the hammer back to half-cock. Then he tore open the cartridge, put the ball in his mouth and poured the powder from the barrel, spilling a little. He balled up the cartridge paper and after briefly raising the gun to let the powder fall into place, rammed the wad home, spat the ball in, and rammed that home too. With some rifles you had to hammer the ball down the rifling but this gun had been used so often the worn rifling provided little resistance.

He took one of the copper caps and fitted it over the nipple. Then he pulled the hammer back to full-cock. Now, providing he didn't point the gun downwards, when the ball might just roll out, he had a loaded weapon. Hell, no wonder the Apaches had lost with guns like these!

There had been no firing from above for a while. The sniper was probably biding his time, maybe refilling his magazine too. He'd also had the chance to line up the space just around the rocks. That first, aimed shot was always dangerous. He needed to be made to waste it again, then Roche could get his own in.

He looked around and found nothing better than a dried-up twig about a foot long. It would have to do. He daren't risk the rifle itself nor even the rammer – without that the rifle was useless. He took off his hat, balanced it on the stick and slowly raised it into plain sight.

The aimed shot was quick and accurate. The hat was torn from the stick and flung back. Good shooting with a Winchester at that range – for all its long barrel it still fired pistol ammunition.

It had been Roche's original intention to risk the sniper's second shot as he raised himself to fire but he thought better of it. Instead he drew the .32, raised it just above the rock and fired blind, twice.

He had no chance of hitting anything but nothing disturbed the aim like being fired back at. The three returned shots proved that, only one hitting the rock, the other two a yard short and well to the side.

Now or never, Roche thought. He lifted his barrel over the rock and sighted on the man 150 yards off. The temptation to pull the trigger early was enormous but he didn't yield to it. He saw the man was too exposed, as if he knew his intended victim didn't have a long arm to fire back at him. Maybe he supposed the rifle to be a shotgun. But once he'd fired the rifle, the sniper would know for certain and—

Crack! The hammer came down on the cap and the gun pushed at his shoulder with twice the force of a modern Springfield as the spinning ball made its way towards the sniper above. Roche didn't try to see if he'd hit anything, just got down behind the rock again, now clouded with gunsmoke. He'd heard no cry but he'd been temporarily deafened by the report of his own gun. All the same, he felt sure he'd hit him.

Feeling something and being right about it were two different things. Roche started to reload. It went much quicker the second time, though this time he didn't raise the barrel to get the powder down. He couldn't risk the gun. All the same, he doubted a second shot would be needed.

It was very quiet. There had been no answering fire. Somebody up there, knowing now they were up against a rifle, ought to be wasting a few bullets in the hope of a ricochet. But nothing.

All the same, he didn't raise his head over the rock. He got to his knees, holding the gun, and came out from behind the rocks, rolling a couple of yards from it and then bringing the weapon to bear.

He didn't fire. He could see him, lying on the high ground, the glittering barrel of the Winchester at his feet, the colour of blood on his shirt and darkening the ground around him.

Roche sighed, went back to collect his hat and the .32 which he'd dropped behind the rock, then looked for his horse. Amazingly it had scarcely moved from where he'd left it, at the other side of the pass, seemingly unconcerned. As if it had known no one was shooting at it. All the same he approached it slowly, rubbing its nose gently as he came close, to calm it in case appearances were deceptive.

'Sorry, jughead,' he said unfairly, but then the horse only heard the tone. He stashed his rifle back in the saddle sheath and mounted up. If the ball fell out now, it scarcely mattered.

He rode past the spot where the sniper lay above him, looking for his horse. He found it a hundred yards further in, hidden by a twist in the ever-narrowing pass, its reins tied off to a stunted bush growing out of the side of the pass. He tied off his own horse and walked up the same trail the sniper had taken. It was easy going and he took his time.

'You were lucky,' Harry Quinn said.

'I had a rifle. A poor one but a rifle will beat a carbine every time.'

'You'd only a shotgun when you left the Bar Q.'

'Things change. How did you know I'd be coming here?'

Harry Quinn spat blood, then: 'I didn't. I knew you'd talked to Carlito. In Spanish. Nobody knew what he might have said. I couldn't take the chance.' He broke off for a moment, then: 'Hell, it's starting to hurt!'

'Tell me about Lucie.'

'She's back there, safe and sound. Hell, I didn't intend to hurt her or her mother. I just stopped to make her an offer. She went mad – screamed at me that I'd murdered her husband. She grabbed my gun, we fought for it and it went off. The kid saw it all.'

'You had a witness then.'

'Yeah, but in town she'd say "Harry Quinn shot my mother", and it wouldn't have mattered a damn that I owned the sheriff – always a sad bargain – I'd still end up swinging from a tree. Damn it, they already reckon every disaster in the county is my work if I buy up land after it. A feller gets snake-bit, the Bar Q's responsible. I never murdered anybody, Roche.'

'Not even Templeton? He was a good horseman.'

'When he was sober. Hell, you've seen the ranch. It just isn't viable on its own.'

Roche found he believed him. 'And?'

'I thought you'd get tired, go away. You didn't. But you couldn't hurt me, not unless you came here, found Lucie, so … Hell, I'm dying, ain't I?'

The bullet had pierced the lower lobe of the left lung and touched the spine too. The unseen exit wound from the 50-calibre ball would be huge. Whatever else, he'd die of sheer blood loss. Roche nodded.

'Better'n hanging, I suppose,' Quinn said. He was silent a moment. 'Tell 'em all what I said. I never killed nobody. I'm sorry about the girl but she'd have been looked after. What's she to you, anyway?'

'My daughter,' Roche said.

Quinn coughed up blood. 'Hell, I didn't ...' He coughed up more blood and then it was all over. Roche turned and walked down the same way he had come.

The pueblo wasn't hard to find. No one had concealed the trail to it, and if it wasn't on the map, it wasn't out of secrecy but from its sheer insignificance. The 'houses' were set in the same grid pattern as Pueblo Viejo but weren't adobe, nor even truly houses – just wickiups with stones round their bases. The sunlight was slanting down on them – they were on the reverse slope, as he'd guessed – but the reddening light added no glamour to the desolate assemblage.

A man stepped forth from the nearest wickiup and walked slowly towards him. Roche had reloaded his .32 on the way here but he knew now it wouldn't be needed. The chief was ancient, dressed American-fashion except for a sombrero of some decrepitude. He stopped several paces away.

"You have come for the *señorita*?'

Roche nodded.

'And Señor Quinn?'

'Dead.'

The old man shook his head.

'Ay, Chihuahua, I taught him to ride, *señor*. Maybe not a good man but not all bad, I—'

'You're Domingo?'

'*Sí, señor.*'

'There's no need to overdo the Mexican business,' Roche said, dismounting. 'I know who you really are. In a way, Carlito sent me here.' He paused, then: 'I mean you no harm.'

'And yet, if you use the word "Apaches", they will drive us all to the reservation, maybe kill us.'

'The hell with them!' Roche said. 'All I care about is the girl. She's well?'

'She's with the women.'

'Call for her.'

Domingo called, not in Spanish but in Apache, a few short staccato words. But they served their purpose. A woman appeared at the doorway of one of the furthest wickiups, ushering forth a child.

Roche didn't move, just stared at her. The clothes were still American but ragged and dirty now. The pueblo wasn't a very clean place. Her hair had been braided and darkened with fat but her eyes were a startling blue.

The woman brought her right up to him, then turned and left. Lucie just looked up at him, a little diffidently but without fear. He could see that they had treated her well, as one of their own.

'You're Lucie, aren't you?'

She nodded.

'I've come for you.' He'd intended to add, to take you back home, but perhaps 'home' wasn't quite the word to use. That dilapidated ranch was only one step up from this forsaken place.

'Who're you?'

Roche looked down at the small face, still chubby though the cheeks were smudged with soot. Any doubts he'd harboured were now gone. Slowly, so as not to frighten her, he knelt down to face her.

'My name's Philip Roche,' he said slowly. 'I'm your new daddy. I ...' He broke off and then decided to use the word anyway, 'I've come to take you home.' He put out his hand to her.

She hesitated, sucking her thumb, then:

'My daddy's dead.'

'But I'm your real daddy. You're my daughter, Lucie. I've come to take care of you.' And suddenly he was weeping silently, the tears running down his cheeks. And he was unashamed.

Lucie reached out and touched his hand.

'It's good cheese,' Domingo said, crumbling it in his fingers to aid his few remaining teeth. He really was a very old man. Outside, standing, the dignity showed through but sitting by the fire in the wick-iup every crease was highlighted and shadowed by the smoky light and his age and weakness were well to the fore.

'Army cheese,' Roche said.

'Good cheese is good cheese,' Domingo said, finishing it. 'You're sure you don't want to leave Quinn here in the hills?'

He'd already sent two boys to collect the body. It was now lying, wrapped in deerskin, in one of the unused wickiups. His horse stood outside, waiting fruitlessly.

'Take it to the Bar Q and tell them what happened. They'll believe you.'

'Yeah, I've worked for them long enough.'

'Even when you were working for the Templetons?'

Domingo grinned, rather grotesquely. 'Yeah, I got double pay then – more from the Bar Q than them. Templeton didn't have much money and Mrs Templeton was mighty tight with it.'

'You saw the killing,' Roche said softly, glancing down at Lucie asleep by the fire, wrapped in a blanket.

'She tried to kill him,' Domingo said. 'He didn't lie. Never killed nobody either. He was hard but only with money – as tight as Mrs Templeton with that, except he had more of it. I reckon that was his real fault, greed. Especially for land.'

'He also said Templeton was a drunk.'

Domingo shrugged. 'He drank some. Couldn't altogether blame him. Truth is, Mrs Templeton was a bit of a shrew. They were always arguing ... usually about her.' He nodded at the small, sleeping form. 'They had some dispute about...'

'Paternity?'

'Yeah. And, of course, about money too. She was no more cut out to be a rancher's wife than he was to be a rancher. Hell, none of this would have happened if

Harry Quinn hadn't offered her just fifteen hundred for the ranch. She was as angry about that as Templeton's death. But then I reckon deep down she half-guessed he was drunk at the time, just couldn't admit it.'

'I thought Quinn had sent Morton to kill me too.'

'Ha, a real sidewinder that. He didn't need anyone to get him to do someone a bad turn. He knew the sheriff wouldn't push it afterwards – glad to have no competition again.'

Roche shook his head. 'A lot of people have died since I came here.'

'Quinn's fault. He saw a way of saving money. With the girl out of the way he thought he'd pick up the ranch for the payment of back taxes. Didn't know about the will till later.'

'And you went along with it.'

'No choice. If he'd let on we're Apaches – well, you know what happened to Carlito. And you did him a good turn too, I hear.'

'They'd no call to hang him.'

'Don't blame 'em. You can't trust Mimbreños. I've fought with 'em and against 'em in the old days and never trusted 'em either way. Then the Quinns came. We had a few Mex guns and our bows. They'd Colts and long rifles. They drove us off our land.'

'Your pueblo.'

'Yeah, the Bar Q ranch house. You noticed.'

'Like Pueblo Viejo, a grid pattern, easy to defend. The Quinns filled in the gaps, added another storey.'

'Yeah, we were settled down when they came – too small a tribe even then to live by just raiding, though we still did some. After we fought the Quinns – and Old Man Quinn was one hard *hombre* – we were pretty much just women and kids. So we reached an accommodation... That's how the Bar Q ranch grew when others didn't: Apache wranglers and hands working for just food and blankets. Later, some of us worked in town but calling ourselves Mexicans. Better to be a Mexican than an Apache.' He paused, looked long at Roche, then:

'You're going to tell?'

'If I say "yes"?'

'Nothing. There's enough to explain already with Harry Quinn dead. With two white men dead...'

'I won't tell, you have my word on it,' Roche said. He paused. 'I suppose things will be easier for you under William Quinn.'

Domingo laughed. 'Heck, he'll leave the running to Helen, nothing's more sure.'

'She knows about you?'

'Not really. Oh, she's heard the myth but she's never thought about it, never had to. The Quinn brothers were always close-mouthed, about that especially.' He paused. 'Hell, what's to know? That we're not Zuñis or some other kind of Pueblo Indians but Apaches? Not any longer. We live like Pueblo Indians or Mexicans, even think like 'em. So what is the difference?'

Roche shrugged, then 'She'll take her uncle's death badly.'

'Reckon so.' Domingo paused. 'I hear tell she thinks highly of you.'

Roche looked at him.

The ancient laughed. 'I've got spies in Bar Q – all those "Mexican" servants. One's my daughter. She don't miss much either. Even reckoned it went both ways.'

'Maybe it did,' Roche admitted.

'And now?'

'I killed her uncle. She loved him like a father.'

'Can't gainsay that. But women are funny creatures...' He paused. 'If'n you want, I can say it was a stray Mimbreño killed him. With a wound like that maybe they'll believe it.'

'I keep your secret, you keep mine?'

'Sometimes pays to have insurance. As I said, it's way better to be a Mex than an Apache.'

Roche was silent.

'It seems to me, what Helen Quinn doesn't know about, she doesn't worry about. Maybe it would be better that way. And your secret would be kept. We're still Apache enough for that.'

Roche considered a few moments longer then shook his head. 'I've got my daughter. That's enough.'

'She really is yourn?'

Roche nodded.

'You going to tell her that.'

Roche thought about it. He didn't need to. What had been said earlier could still be disregarded. Legally there was no problem at all. The will made him her guardian and nobody would care anyway. But he was sick of lies. He'd keep Domingo's secret because it wasn't his to divulge but as for the rest, damn all lies.

'Yes.' Domingo nodded. 'I reckon she'll grow up right proud.'

8

Roche lay back on the bunk in the jail cell and read the headlines of the *Lanchester City & County News*, holding the slim paper above his head:

HERO OF CARLITO BATTLE

RECOVERS TEMPLETON CHILD

May Stand for County Sheriff

He balled up the paper and threw it across the cell. The 'Templeton Child' reference annoyed him especially – Walters had refused to print that she was his blood-daughter.

'You don't put that kind of thing in cold print,' he'd said.

So much for his determination to have no more lies....

The bit about standing for sheriff was pure nonsense – Walters was trying to put pressure on him. Much good would it do him. As soon as Lucie was fit for the stage journey, they were going back East. Mrs Pequod, the pastor's wife, had insisted Lucie would need at least several weeks to regain her 'equanimity', whatever that meant in a five-year-old child.

He'd intended to stay at the hotel but the town had virtually insisted on lionizing him and the Pequods had the requisite two spare rooms.

He sighed. He was too old for dull meals, long graces before them and uplifting conversation. At least Lucie seemed to be enjoying it all, though. They were fitting her for new dresses now. Fortunately he was still marshal so he had been able to make his excuse and beat a retreat from the house.

He was lost in his thoughts and didn't

hear Andrews enter, only noticed him when his shadow touched the bottom of the bunk.

'You've left the key in the cell door,' the lawyer said. 'Someone could lock you in.'

Roche drew his .32 and levelled it. 'I'd only shoot them if they did.'

For a moment Andrews was taken aback, then he shook his head. 'Foolishness aside, I've business with you, Marshal.'

Roche reholstered the gun. Andrews was right. He wasn't about to shoot anyone. 'Go on.'

'I'd be obliged if you'd come out of there.'

Roche sighed again. A lawyer ought to be used to talking to people in cells but there was no use saying that or even arguing. He just didn't intimidate them any more. He was an official hero and heroes are public property. It was best simply to put up with it, especially as he would be leaving soon.

'So what is it?' he asked, reaching the desk and gesturing Andrews to the visitor's chair he'd had brought in.

'The Bar Q won't buy the Templeton ranch.'

'You went down to three thousand dollars?'

'Money wasn't discussed. They just won't buy.'

'So sell to someone else.'

'There are no other takers at that price.'

'Reduce it.'

'No use, nobody in town is about to make an enemy of the Bar Q.'

'So it doesn't get sold,' Roche said. 'It will eventually. I'll give you power of attorney—'

'I don't believe it will but there's more. The Bar Q wishes to discuss the matter with you, personally.'

'William Quinn's in your office?' Roche asked, getting to his feet.

'Miss Quinn's in my house. It's rather more private than my office. She came there from the Pequods.' He paused. 'I must say, she seemed rather angry.'

'I killed her uncle.'

'Regrettable, but that was almost an accident.'

'No, it wasn't,' Roche began and stopped. Andrews knew the truth already. If he and the town wanted a sanitized version of recent history, let them have it. He'd be gone soon enough.

'I won't accompany you, sir. She speci-
fied that she wanted to see you alone.'

She was wearing the same dress he'd seen
her in that first time, when he'd retrieved
her errant hatbox. She was seated by the
fireplace in Andrews' dining-room. She
didn't speak when Mr Andrews' house-
keeper admitted him, waiting for her to
close the door behind her. Then:

'Red Walters says you're taking Lucie
back East.'

'Yes,' Roche said. 'I—'

'You were going to leave without a
word.'

'I thought it best. Your uncle—'

'He was my uncle. He's buried now. I
loved him but he was wrong.' She paused.
'I went to where he died. I saw the pueblo.
I'd never seen it before and I didn't realize. Now I'm bringing them south. There's
no need for people to have to live like that
and...' She broke off.

'I'm pleased,' Roche said.

She looked down at her hands in
silence. Then, suddenly:

'Don't you realize I'm ashamed for what

was done to Lucie? And did you think that I'd think less of her knowing she's your daughter?'

'No.'

'You were going to go back East without a word to me, weren't you? You know how I feel about you but—'

'I killed—'

'Enough of killing! What's done is done. I know you had no choice. And it's now that matters. Look at you, hiding in the marshal's office! A man alone can't see to a child. You'd have gone back East and married a barmaid just to have someone for her—'

'I wouldn't have married a barmaid,' Roche said patiently.

'But you would have married someone you didn't love!'

Roche realized he'd had a choice once, maybe when he'd received the lawyer's letter. Yes, he could have ignored it and gone on as before. But since he'd come out West he'd had no real choices at all. Just things he had to do because they had to be done.

Like now.

And he was deeply grateful for it.

He went to her, took her by the shoulders and lifted her to her feet.

'There's no chance of that now,' he said and kissed her through her tears.

EPILOGUE

Domingo looked out to the south from the Tenit Hills. 'Tenit' was the name of his tribe and also meant 'separated', rather than 'hidden' in their Apache dialect. No matter. It was a word that would soon be lost.

Already the Tenit Apaches were losing their old language and not for Spanish either, but for English. Domingo spoke all three tongues but he didn't regret the change. Language was just a tool. Only a fool used an inappropriate tool.

The Chiricahua Apaches had fought and found themselves in far Florida for their pains; other tribes languished in reservations, like steers hemmed in by the newfangled barbed wire, which he had heard talk of but never seen. It was two wires twisted together to hold wire barbs, an ingenious idea like so many of those of the white men from the East, whose numbers would have been too great to oppose even if their weapons hadn't been so superior.

Better not to fight a doomed war even if it meant the young men of the tribe were no longer warriors. At last they were alive.

He would be the last chief of the Tenit Apaches, for there was no one to follow him. He had sons but such authority as he had was now personal, not to be inherited.

In all truth the man who ran the Bar Q would be more their chief than anyone and in that they were lucky. Harry Quinn had been a hard man but while Roche was harder, he was a man of honour too. He would keep his word, which was the heart and soul of honour. Besides which, Domingo liked him. There was no cruelty in him, and that was to the good.

There had been cruelty in the old ways. Perhaps of necessity, for it was a cruel land, but maybe the way of the white incomers was best, not trying to match the land but to master it.

That went dead against the old ways; the medicine men would have condemned him out of hand for saying it but the last of them had died ten years ago and he was himself too old now to love land for itself or to worship it. People mattered, not land. They couldn't live without it but it was still secondary. And his people would live.

If not himself. It was near the time when this old body would put off warmth and movement for cold and stillness, and he found he did not mind overmuch. He had lived a long life, seen many things. In his youth he had raided in Mexico with the Mimbreños, fought the Mexicans and, once, the Yaquis. He had known three wives, all good women, and his sons were many.

If they weren't warriors in the old way they were yet free men, not like the Chiricahua or the White Mountain Apaches who lived where they were told and ate watered army beef. His sons carried guns and rode fine horses and were respected.

What if they no longer worshipped in

the Old Way? The old customs and beliefs were just tools for living and they had failed. Better to worship the god of the white man who had strength still.

As for himself, he fell between stools. He scarcely believed he would ride the white horse into the lands of summer, nor the stories of the white preachermen who promised much the same even if their way of obtaining it was somewhat different. He noticed that the white men too were less than anxious to test the validity of their promise.

No matter. The world was strange and deceptive and maybe there was more held inside this old frame than tired blood and weary bones. He hoped so. Whatever, he, Domingo, who had once been called Wolf in the Night, Chief of the Tenits, had served his people as well as he knew how. They would forget him but that too was good, for in the old ways a warrior should be forgotten when he died.

Was the white of the Bar Q turning a little golden? He glanced to the west and saw the first streaks of red in the sky. Time to go back while there was still light. Death would take him soon enough without his active aid, and there was food and warmth in the wickiup and a woman to lie with, and if she matched his years, that too was fitting.

Domingo climbed wearily down but with the adeptness of long practice and a heart at peace. The last chief of the Tenit Apaches had done his whole duty.